HUMAN JACKALS

Without hesitation, Ki spun. Half a dozen rough-dressed men were approaching from the rear. Several carried clubs. Seeing him turn, they spread out and approached in a semicircle of gap-toothed grins.

He picked out the smallest of the half-dozen. A bandy-legged man with a red bandanna knotted around his dirty throat, darted at him.

Bandy-legs carried a piece of planking. As Ki charged him, his eyes widened, and he threw the board up defensively before his face. Ki broke it with a downward knife-hand, smashed the man's mouth to red ruin with a straight punch from the other hand . . .

— WESLEY ELLIS —

LONE STAR

AND THE TEMPERANCE ARMY

J

JOVE BOOKS, NEW YORK

LONE STAR AND THE TEMPERANCE ARMY

A Jove Book / published by arrangement with the author

PRINTING HISTORY
Jove edition / January 1995

ISBN: 0-515-11529-0

A JOVE BOOK®
Jove Books are published by The Berkley Publishing Group,
200 Madison Avenue, New York, New York 10016.
JOVE and the "J" design are trademarks
belonging to Jove Publications, Inc.

PRINTED IN THE UNITED STATES OF AMERICA

10 9 8 7 6 5 4 3 2 1

LONE STAR

AND THE
TEMPERANCE ARMY

Chapter 1

"This land oppresses me," Ki said, gesturing out the stagecoach window with a calloused brown hand. It was as hard a hand as any a man might expect to find in the West. But if a body examined it up close, he might notice the calluses weren't quite the same as you'd find on the hands of your run-of-the-mill wrangler, miner, or sodbuster.

"You always say that," Jessica Starbuck said with one of her patented radiant smiles, "whenever we come to Kansas."

If the jolting of the iron-bound wheels over the parallel collection of ruts called the road could be felt through the wagon's springs, through the inadequate padding of the seats, through the somewhat more stylish padding of her rump to her tailbone, she never showed it. Jessie Starbuck was truly her father's daughter. She had been raised to appreciate comfort, but not to expect it. And she knew in her bones what so many in her privileged position forgot or never knew: that the comfort and plenty available to her as heir to the worldwide Starbuck trading empire could only be maintained by sweat, endurance, and, at need, the headlong readiness to risk her neck.

1

And indeed, there was more to risk her neck for than prosperity: there was pride. In herself, in her heritage, in the loyalty she commanded, as her father had, from every one of myriad Starbuck employees. Her father, Alex Starbuck, had been a proud man who never swerved from doing what he saw as the right thing.

It had gotten him killed. That didn't deter Jessie. Alex would have said that was a fitting way for a man to die, and she agreed.

So she didn't mind a few shocks to the tailbone. Nor the uncompromising flatness of central Kansas in the lead-sheet heat of a summer morning.

"I am accustomed to more varied surroundings," the tall man said. "There is little here to please the eye."

"You pride yourself on being a warrior," she said in a friendly bantering tone. "Show some of that warrior's endurance."

"A true warrior cultivates his taste for beauty as he cultivates his skill at arms."

"Well, why don't you appreciate the simple austere beauty, like those sand gardens the monks have in their Zen monasteries back in the Japans?"

"I am not a monk."

"*That's* the truth," she said.

Teeth gleamed white in his tan face. He laughed. Jessie's bodyguard could seem grim as a stone statue or pompous as a bishop, but his moods tended to flash by like the cloud shadows sliding over the wheatfields. One consistent trait was his sense of humor, though strong, understated, and slightly skewed.

The stagecoach was full of the smells of leather, varnish, trail dust, old human sweat, and the team of horses straining up front. It seemed to consist entirely of its springs, loose joints, and metal fittings on the harness and frame, which groaned and clattered and jingled in a constant not-quite-rhythmic concert punctuated by hoof thunder, the soft grunting of the horses, and the driver's cries. The great wheels ran in ruts laid down by heavily

2

laden wagons, which tended to keep it headed in the right direction. But every now and then they would introduce a tooth-jarring lurch, causing the cabin to fill with dust motes swarming like gnats in the sunlight streaming in the window and making everything rattle like a barrelful of cutlery rolling down the cellar stairs.

"I remember when I was a little girl," Jessie said. "That town we got off the train in used to be named Busted Straight." She shook her head. "Now it's got to calling itself Pleasant View."

"That seems overly optimistic," Ki said.

"That's smalltown boosterism for you. The city fathers catch the respectability bug and forget where they came from."

"Some have that luxury," he said.

She glanced at him. He was looking out the far window at the telegraph poles ticking past, which was at least an added element to the monotony. From the angle he looked like any other Westerner: a tall, spare-built man, with black hair hanging to broad shoulders, dressed in dusty denim pants, a loose shirt, and a leather vest.

But his eyes, turned away for the moment, were anything but typical. Their almond shape gave away the Japanese half of his ancestry. He was a man with his feet in two worlds and a place in neither. He endured, because he really was a warrior, but Jessie knew it wasn't easy for him.

Two thumps of a stage gun butt sounded on the roof, and then the shotgun man was leaning precariously over to yell in, "Center City's just up ahead, ma'am!"

It wasn't actually necessary for the shotgun rider to lean way over to yell, unless he wanted to see in. Jessie Starbuck was well worth the risk. She was tall and her hair was blond that glinted with a hint of copper in the sun, and her face was the sort to keep a man awake in his bedroll nights. The conservative pale-green jacket she wore over a silken blouse the color of fresh cream and the long green skirt only hinted at the figure beneath, but any man with red blood in his veins had to like the directions those hints were taking.

3

She smiled and nodded. "Thank you, Scooter." Her voice was cheerful, but there was just that ring to it, like a silver dollar dropped on a bar, that didn't encourage the shotgun rider to keep gawking at her like a prize heifer. His face bobbed acknowledgment and bounced up out of sight.

The smile faded from her face. A certain tightness had gathered in the pit of her unfashionably flat belly. This was not a pleasure trip.

Though in her constant travels with her father, Jessie had been through the railway town of Busted Straight, now Pleasant View, she had never before been to Center City. It was home to a most minor outpost of the farflung Starbuck empire: the Liberty Saloon, won by Alex Starbuck in a Kansas City poker game. It was not the sort of operation which would normally command the attention of the head of the whole big show.

But Jessie had gotten a frantic telegram for help from the Liberty's proprietor, a man named Brian Denning. And that was another part of the Starbuck pride—and the glue that held the empire together. She demanded absolute loyalty from her employees, but she gave them nothing less in return. If they needed help, they got it.

Besides, she thought with a quirky little grin, *it keeps life interesting.*

"Interesting" was not a name she would hang on Center City, Kansas, she thought as they rolled through the outskirts. Likely Ki wouldn't either, but he had lapsed into one of his thoughtful silences, where he seemed to be a million miles away. They had started seeing the occasional house, as opposed to sodbuster burrows, next to lines of trees planted as windbreaks. Now they were rolling and banging along among the usual shanty-scattered outskirts of town, inhabited by those the good folk didn't want to brush elbows with. Then they were surrounded by the usual prim whitewashed Victorian houses and false-front buildings of Center City proper.

The middle of Center City was a neat little square, with elm trees lining the sidewalk and a captive Confederate

4

howitzer parked out in front of a white gazebo. The road ran on south, across the north fork of Jericho Creek, swollen by late-season runoff from the distant Rockies, and then straight as a gunshot ten miles to Williams. Customarily the stage stopped in front of the Center City Hotel to discharge passengers and take on new.

But there was nobody waiting today, and besides, Jessie Starbuck just tended to get that extra little bit of service. Ernie Phillips, the driver, knew she was headed down to take charge of the Liberty—an establishment not unfamiliar to him or his shotgun partner, Scooter Longmire—so he kept the horses whipped up and trotting the two extra blocks toward the saloon.

Or that was his intent. Almost as soon as it passed the square the stagecoach began to rattle to a stop with a squeal of brakes and a "Whoa!" from Phillips. At the same time Ki stiffened and frowned.

Jessie stuck her head out the window. "What's the matter?"

The driver's bearded face peered down at her. "Looks like trouble down at the Liberty, ma'am."

A block and a half ahead, a crowd of a dozen or so was milling outside swinging doors that led into the corner of a three-story white building. She could hear angry shouts, and realized that they were what had caused her bodyguard to go on the alert.

"Drive on," she said, "slowly."

The driver moistened his lips with a pale tongue, nodded, shook the reins, and clucked the horses to a walk.

"Jessie—"

"Don't worry, Ki," she said. "I'm not going to go charging into the middle of things."

"When did you experience this change of heart?"

She made a face at him. Then a change in the noise of the crowd made her look out again.

The men before the double doors were in violent motion now, jostling each other to get closer to the flurry of arms and legs she could see at the middle. They were really whooping

5

each other on now, alternating curses and laughter.

"Stop the coach," Jessie commanded. It complied, complaining. She stepped down into the street without waiting for Ernie to finish scrambling down to help her.

"You boys stay here," she said. "You don't need any part of this." And she marched toward the crowd.

Ki said something in Japanese and followed her. He had to step pretty briskly to keep up; much of Jessie's height was in her legs.

"I thought you weren't going to rush into anything," he said.

"Things changed, kind of sudden."

Nobody was paying them any mind. As they got close, the crowd abruptly parted. A figure staggered out. Its face was a shiny mask of blood, its clothes torn and sodden. It took three steps toward Jessie, held out mashed fingers, and dropped to its knees.

★
Chapter 2

Disregarding her outfit, Jessie cradled the man's head on her knee. Breath bubbled unevenly from a toothless gape of mouth. Pink froth ran down his chin. He was in a bad way.

The crowd closed in. Jessie froze them with a glare. "Get back."

"Mind your own business, sister," said a man who had one eye that looked at random off across the county.

"Yeah," snarled a beefy, redfaced man behind him. "We're doing the Lord's work here."

"It looks like coward's work to me!" she snapped. "All you against one man."

"Look here, Miss Fancy-Pants," sneered the man with the wandering eye, "I'll teach you to open that smart mouth of yours to men of God!"

He aimed a slap at her face. Another hand darted in to intercept his. Without seeming to rush, Ki had stepped forward and grabbed it.

The bodyguard twisted it back. "Yow, my hand! You're busting my hand!" the man yelped.

Ki shrugged, released the hand—and slammed a savage *teisho* palm-heel strike into his nose.

The man reeled back, clutching a nose that gushed like an oil rig. "Yow, my nose! You busted my nose!"

"It is the part of wisdom," Ki told him, "to know when one is well-off."

"Lousy chili-belly bastard!" the beefy, redfaced man yelled. He put his head down and rushed at Ki, arms outstretched to grab. Ki stood waiting. Just as the bigger man reached him in his all-out bullmoose rush, he grabbed him by one wrist and pivoted away from him, sliding out a foot as he did so. The redfaced man tripped, fell heavily, and went rolling along the street like a horizontal avalanche until his head cracked against the watering trough on the sidestreet next to the saloon. Water sloshed over him. He lay moaning, holding his head.

Another burly specimen seized Ki from behind in a bear hug, and picked him up off the ground. A towheaded man, grinning, closed in to drive a punch into Ki's unprotected belly. Ki's right foot, encased in a cork-soled black slipper, snapped out to catch him in the groin with the instep. The impact raised the man four fingers off the dusty road. When he came back down he crumpled.

The crowd was beginning to break up. They were obviously out for a little good clean *fun*. They hadn't bargained on anything nasty happening, like running into someone who could defend himself. But one or two, encouraged by Ki's predicament, lunged forward past Jessie to get in on the entertainment.

Her left leg shot out and scythed one's legs out from under him. He squealed like a pig as front teeth snapped on the hard-packed dirt of the street. Another, frustrated fury overcoming his loutish concept of chivalry, aimed a stiff-legged kick at her face. She leaned back away from the kick, caught the man by the heel with her right hand, and pulled him toward her. At the same time she drove her left hand hard into his crotch.

"That'll teach you to take liberties with a lady," she said

primly as he collapsed, hunched over himself.

Ki snapped his head back, mashing the nose of the man who held him. Squalling, the man let go and tried to leap back. Reaching back, Ki grabbed his head. Then he jackknifed forward, pitching the burly man over his shoulder—and right into the face of yet another charging assailant. Both went down in a tangle.

Ki sprang to stand protectively over Jessie, who had managed to keep from letting the injured man's head slide from her knee. But the crowd had had more than enough fun. It was dissolving down the streets and melting into alleys, the former combatants picking themselves up and limping in the rear.

"Dogs," Ki said conversationally. He dusted his hands.

"You want us to go fetch a doctor for that poor fella, ma'am?" asked Scooter, the beanpole shotgun rider. He and his partner had come up to lend a hand despite Jessie's warning. They hadn't felt needed.

Slowly Jessie eased the beaten man's head to the road. Then she stood, anger flaming in her green eyes. Her fine blouse was red with a shocking smear of blood.

"It's too late," she said bitterly. "He's dead."

"A man has been murdered, Chief Coates," Jessie said crisply. "I want to know what you intend to do about it."

The chief of police for Center City gazed at her for a moment from watery blue eyes, then put a hand on the green baize blotter of his desktop for help in the considerable task of hoisting his blue-clad brass-buttoned belly out from behind it. Then he rose and went to stare out the window at the square, through the branches of one of the imported plane trees which flanked the courthouse steps.

He clasped hands behind his back and bobbed on the balls of his feet, perhaps harkening back to the big city beat-cop he had likely once been. "You got any guns?"

"I beg your pardon?"

He looked at her. She was seated before the desk in the cheery little office, with Ki standing behind her. "I asked

9

you if you or this Mexican feller was carrying any firearms, Miss Starbuck."

"What on earth has that got to do with anything?" she demanded.

"It's against the law for private citizens to carry firearms within the confines of Center City," Chief Coates said.

She waved a hand at Ki. "Do you see any guns?"

"Nooo."

Jessie felt the cool hardness of the ivory-handled .38 derringer worn in a garter against her right thigh. She felt no guilt at her failure to mention it.

A whine edged into his voice: "You needn't take that tone with me, Miss Starbuck. We can't be too careful. If we don't watch out we'll have armed bands of maniacs running wild in the streets, committin' acts of indecency against the citizens."

"Chief Coates," Jessie said, speaking to him slowly and distinctly, as she might to a none-too-swift child, "a man lies dead in Dr. Hargrove's parlor. I want to know what you intend to do about it."

He turned to face her, bobbing his head up and down in its nest of chins. "A man lies dead," he said gravely. "But we do things proper in Center City, ma'am. Before we go racing off in all directions and jumping at conclusions, we conduct an investigation. That is what I propose to do: *investigate.*"

"Investigate?" She jumped to her feet. The Chief cowered back. She was taller by two inches. "*Investigate?* What is there to investigate? The man was *murdered,* Chief. I saw it happen."

"You saw the man *die,* Miss Starbuck," Coates said. Sweat was strung along his far-receded hairline like a chain. "That doesn't mean there was murder done. No, indeed. There are still a good many questions to be answered."

"Such as what?"

"Such as whether the death occurred as a result of violence, as you believe—and, ma'am, permit me to say I do not for one moment doubt your sincerity. But I've been

10

dealing with witnesses all my life, and one thing I've learned is that even the sincerest and best intentioned among them is often confused by the rapid course of events."

"What else *could* have happened?"

"Well, as I see it, it's possible your man injured himself through some misadventure, a fall from a ladder, perhaps. This happened by chance at the same time as the boisterous activity you described going on at the Liberty Saloon—though why a woman of your obvious quality should be troubling herself about the affairs of such a sordid den is as big a mystery to me as anything, ma'am."

"I own it," she said tautly.

His eyebrows rose and he bounced on his feet some more. "I see. I see. Well, it's clear that this will take some looking into. Now, if you will be so kind as to excuse me, young lady—"

On the courthouse steps Ki said, "Is that why your countrymen so frequently depict Justice wearing a blindfold?"

"Very funny." She looked down at herself. Her clothing was beyond recovery. The blood was beginning to turn rank in the sticky Kansas heat. "Let's get back to the Liberty and see what pieces we can pick up. And I'm dying to change—I'm about to steam to death in all this wool."

The Liberty looked as if it had hosted simultaneous reunions of both armies of Northern Virginia, McClellan's and Hill's. A half-dozen employees had emerged from hiding and stood blinking around as if in shock. Having made sure that no one else was injured, Jessie left Ki to take charge of the situation while she swept upstairs to change.

A few minutes later she came back down, dressed in her usual working outfit: a light blue man's shirt, faded jeans, and cowboy boots. Undoubtedly the proper women of Center City would elevate their noses at her for dressing like a common laborer. Right now she didn't care a whole thunderous lot for Center City or the opinions of anybody in it.

A stout man with a moustache and a flowered carpet bag about to burst like an overcooked sausage met her at the foot of the stairs.

"Miss Starbuck?"

She looked at him coolly. "You have the advantage of me, sir."

He blinked, dropped his eyes. "I, uh, I'm sorry, ma'am. I'm Denning. Brian Denning, the, ahh—"

"The manager," she supplied.

He nodded. "I just wanted, ahh, wanted to tell you that I'm, I'm—"

She resisted the urge to grab him by his cravat and shake him. "Yes?"

"—leaving. I quit."

"What?" Jessie said.

"I, I know I sent for you," he said, his pale eyes looking everywhere but at her. "I'm glad you came so quickly. But I—I just didn't bargain for this."

She held out her hands. "I reckon you didn't."

He bobbed his head quickly, seized up his bag, and left.

"Coward," Ki said quietly.

"Don't be so quick to judge," Jessie said, watching the double doors swing back and forth, settling toward rest. "Would you ask him to die for somebody else's place of business?"

"I would."

She looked into his Asian eyes and smiled. "You're not exactly a common man," she said quietly. "And you wouldn't die for just *anybody's* concern . . . would you?"

"No," he acknowledged.

In the corner by the piano a woman was sobbing heartbrokenly. At a nod from his employer, Ki picked his way through broken glass and busted furniture to her. She wore a yellow dress with a low-cut bodice and a lot

12

of crinoline puffing out the skirts. Her hair was a red that seemed to gleam like blood in the dusty afternoon sunlight drifting in from outside.

Ki touched her lightly on the bare shoulder. She jumped, stared up at him with her mouth a startled "O" and her eyes like a frightened pronghorn's.

"Do not fear me," he said. "I am Ki. My employer and I have come to help."

Her face was lovely, with high, fine cheekbones and light hazel eyes. He noticed the way she instinctively ducked, as if to hide the birthmark on her right cheek from him. But she sniffled and smiled bravely.

"I'm Charity Anne House," she said. "I—I'm a dancer here." She shook her head. "What happened is just so horrible. Those Temperance Army people—they act like they're insane!"

Ki frowned and glanced at his employer, who was surveying the bar.

Though his face didn't show it, his spirit was troubled. He hoped Jessie knew what she was getting herself into.

The piano player's paper collar hung open, partially detached from his shirt, his greying blond, disheveled hair hung in his pale narrow face, and he stank abominably of gin. But his eyes and voice were clear, as if a brush with a murderous mob had had a sobering effect.

"The inhabitants of this fair town," he said in an English accent Jessie was reasonably sure was genuine, "have little love for us, it's true. But the ruffians who killed poor Bryce and made such a fearful mess of the place were largely from other venues."

Jessie frowned. "Do you know, Miss Starbuck," the Englishman said, "a little 'vee' appears between your brows when you do that. Most fetching, really."

"Thank you, Mr. Cordwainer. Now, maybe you can tell me as how people are coming from far away to bust up my bar and beat my employees to death."

Pale brows rose in amazement. Though his features

seemed those of a young man, the pallid skin was parchment-dry. "Why they come from all across the length and breadth of this great state of Kansas, Miss Starbuck, as I imagined everybody knew."

"I'm not from around here."

"Ah, forgive me," he said, sweeping his hand theatrically through the air. "Yet I should have thought word of Sister Angela's Divine Temperance Army would have spread far and wide by now, thanks to such modern contrivances as the telegraph. Sister Angela and her Temperance Army have made an almighty splash here in Kansas. I'm surprised the papers elsewhere haven't picked up the tale."

"I don't pay a lot of mind to stories about every two-bit temperance crusader to crop up on the Great Plains, Mr. Cordwainer. Otherwise I wouldn't have time for much else."

"Ah, but Sister Angela is not your *average* temperance crusader, Miss Starbuck," Cordwainer said, shaking his head. "Not by any stretch of the imagination. For one thing, in a few short months she has acquired a following of several hundred, who faithfully follow her anywhere she chooses to take her traveling show; her Temperance Army is an army in more than just name."

He took a grimy handkerchief from the pocket of his black waistcoat and dabbed his face. "Also, Sister Angela is rumored to be a young woman of striking appearance—perhaps even on a par with yours, if one might presume."

"Thank you, sir," Jessie said, repressing a grin. There was a certain exaggerated quality to the piano player's formality of speech and manner that made him seem less pompous than his words sounded. As if he were having constant fun at his own expense.

The impulse to grin didn't hang around long. "Does this Temperance Army go in for this kind of thing often?" she asked, gesturing around at the upturned tables and broken glass.

Cordwainer nodded gravely. "They say they're determined to run the Demon Rum out of Kansas," he said, "if they have to break up every saloon in the state to do it."

"What about murder?"

He compressed his mouth to a line, shook his head. "There have been rumors, certainly, that their methods sometimes have a sinister cast. I confess I was shocked at the brutality they displayed today, though. Poor Bryce."

"Don't the authorities do anything?"

"Ha-ha," he said, feigning laughter. "Sister Angela is highly popular in certain circles; I personally feel certain members of the fair sex are just as happy to see their spouses' favored recreation disrupted. And besides . . ." He clapped one hand over his breast and threw the other one out to the extent of his arm. "What politician would dare to vindicate the right of pathetic rummies such as your humble servant, to go to Perdition in our own way? Saloons are hard to defend, dear lady."

He dropped his arms and shook his head. "And to think," he muttered sadly, "had my father not overlooked the nicety of marrying my mother, I'd be royal astronomer today."

"I'm going to," Jessie stated.

Cordwainer blinked at her owlishly. "Marry my father," he said, "or become royal astronomer?"

"Defend this saloon."

A huge figure loomed up beside them. "Mr. Co'wainer?" it asked in a tentative, thick-tongued voice.

Jessie turned. A mountainous black youth stood there, dressed in overalls and holding a pushbroom.

"Ah, yes, Andy," Cordwainer said. "I'm rather busy now, as you can see—"

"Does this young man work for the Liberty?" Jessie asked.

The youth looked at her, blinked moistly, then looked down at the scuffed toes of his work boots. "Yes, indeed he does," Cordwainer said. "Miss Starbuck, permit me to introduce Andrew McNair. He cleans up for us, does odd jobs."

Jessie stuck out her hand. "I'm pleased to meet you, Andrew."

15

"Hi," Andy said. He scuffed his feet and wouldn't look at her.

"Do shake the lady's hand, there's a good lad," Cordwainer urged.

Shyly Andy reached out, briefly enfolded Jessie's slim hand with his huge chubby one, then quickly broke contact and put his hand behind his back.

"What did you want, Andy?" Jessie asked.

"I—I was wonderin', is Mr. Bryce going to be coming back soon?"

Jessie bit her lip. "No," she said slowly. "He—he's gone away."

Andy was evidently slow, but not *that* slow. He began to cry, very quietly, shoulders shaking and fat tears rolling down his dark round cheeks.

"Andy was very fond of Bryce," Cordwainer explained. "Bryce was able to find rather more time for the lad than most of us."

"Where can I find this Sister Angela?" Jessie asked.

"At the moment, I believe, the Temperance Army is camped outside the town of Williams, south of here."

Jessie nodded. She reached up to pat the weeping Andy on the cheek, then turned to face the room.

"Listen to me," she said. Drawn faces turned toward her. "For those who don't yet know me, my name's Jessie Starbuck. I own the Liberty."

"Reckon you've come to let us all go," a blond woman said bitterly.

"Nobody who doesn't want to go," Jessie said. "I aim to keep the Liberty open."

They stared at her. "You know what you're takin' on, ma'am?" asked a tall balding slat of a man. His right eye was half-shut.

"Reckon I do," Jessie said. "I reckon it's Sister Angela doesn't know what *she's* taking on. So here's my plan: this afternoon we'll work on setting this place to rights. And in the morning I'll ride off to Williams and see what this high-and-mighty Sister thinks she's about."

She put her hands on her hips. "So, who's with me?"

The saloon employees exchanged looks. They were keeping their heads low, like men hunkering behind adobe walls to keep out of Kiowa gunfire.

"If I may be allowed to speak for my associates," Martin Cordwainer said, "they think you're mad. Yet there's no denying it's madness on a magnificent scale."

He stepped forward and stuck out his hand. "I, at least, am your man, Miss Starbuck. I wouldn't miss this show for anything."

One by one the others came forward to touch Jessie's hand. At the back of the bar, Ki stood with arms folded, shaking his head.

★

Chapter 3

"Are you certain this is wise?" Ki asked. He held the reins of the strapping, dark bay gelding Jessie had rented at Bern McAllister's livery stable.

Jessie wore boots and jeans, a blue checked shirt, and her cowboy hat slung over her back. She stuck her foot in the stirrup, grabbed the saddle by horn and cantle, and swung herself abroad. The bay sidestepped and switched its black tail at the flies buzzing in the street outside the Liberty.

"No," she said when she was seated. "I'm just certain it's *right.*"

"You will not permit me to accompany you?" he asked, handing her the reins.

She shook her head firmly. The morning sun struck red highlights like sparks from the hair that bobbed around her shoulders.

"Mr. Cordwainer's stirring speech yesterday not with-standing," she said, "most of our people are nervous as a fawn who just whiffed a puma. They're liable to bolt if somebody doesn't stay and put some starch in their backbones."

She smiled sweetly at her bodyguard. "You're elected."

Ki's handsome face was rebellious. He drew in a breath. Then he closed his mouth on it, nodded, and stood back.

"I'll be fine, Ki," she said. "You worry about me too much."

"I promised your father I would keep you safe," he said. "It is a *giri,* a debt of honor."

"I'll be fine," she said. "Look for me around sundown." She turned the bay's head, nudged him in the ribs, and set off down the street at an easy trot.

A pair of town women were strolling toward her along a section of board sidewalk in front of Sylvester's Millinery. Parasols shaded their heads from the stinging morning sun. Yards of skirt draped over bustles made them seem to glide without moving their feet. Jessie smiled and nodded a good morning to them.

They both looked straight through her. One of them sniffed loudly as she passed.

"Word gets around," Jessie said to herself. She glanced back over her shoulder at the women gliding stiffly away.

Could I really be like them? she wondered. *Would I give myself airs and sniff at anybody who was different from me, if my Daddy had raised me to be a proper little lady?*

The thought gave her a chill. She loved the feel of a good horse between her legs, the hot caress of the sun on her cheek. She could play the lady when it was called for, and even enjoy the role. But as to being like one of those stick-dry prudes—

Never happen. She laughed, tossed her hair, and spurred the bay to a lope.

The land south of Center City wasn't flat, exactly. The land was a slow green roll like the sea on an unusually calm day. There were no trees in sight, nor even bushes, just the endless grassy swells. All that broke up the horizon were cows and the occasional stone fencepost.

The sky was painful blue. A few fat cotton-ball clouds drifted overhead, aimless as the grazing cattle. Near the eastern horizon they were beginning to pile ominously on top of one another. Knowing too well what a sudden plains thunderstorm was like, Jessie resolved to keep half an eye on the budding thunderheads.

The clouds had not yet mounted high enough for their tops to be smeared and flattened out into the characteristic anvil shapes of thunderheads when she spotted the tent city.

At first glimpse it looked like some kind of drover's camp, sprouting from the prairie. But it was too big, a hundred tents at least, interspersed with the occasional knocked-together clapboard shack.

They were wandering among the tents or sitting before them, boiling late coffee over cookfires, playing mumbledy-peg or just chewing the fat. Cards, dice, and bottles of booze were immediately conspicuous by their absence.

Still, the way the men watched Jessie as she rode into the sprawling camp told her that some kinds of sin, at least, were no strangers here.

In the middle of everything rose a big colorful pavilion-style tent that looked as if it might have done time in the circus somewhere along the line. Next to it, a low platform had been cobbled together out of rough undressed pine planking—rare as ivory in this country. A couple of uprights rose from the rear corners. Between them a banner reading SISTER ANGELA'S DIVINE TEMPERANCE ARMY bellied and snapped in the rising breeze.

A couple of strapping young louts jumped up from a pair of overturned buckets beside the entrance to the big tent.

"May I help you, sister?" the towheaded one asked, his eyes starting from his head.

"Morning," she said, reining in. "I'd like to talk to Sister Angela."

The two looked at each other. The blond one licked his lips, looked at her, looked down at his grubby bare feet. "Well, I don't. That is—"

"What's going on here?"

The men lounging around the tent city had been mostly laborers, farmhands, and layabouts, rough in dress and manner. The man who pushed out from under the flap of the pavilion stood out like a swan among crows. He wasn't much by way of size, a skinny stoop-shouldered specimen with glossy dark complexion, black eyes, and reddish-brown sideburns razored to points flanking a wide jaw. What was remarkable was the way he was dressed, in an immaculate, tan three-piece suit with a green foulard and a stickpin boasting a pearl as big as the tip of his thumb. He topped it off with a dark brown bowler hat.

"Mr. Brokaw," the towheaded boy said, "this here lady wants to talk to Sister Angela."

His dark brows came together in a brief frown. Turning to face Jessie, he bowed and doffed the bowler. He had a big head, and its size was exaggerated by the fact that his hairline had retreated almost to the crown, leaving chestnut tufts to either side of a dome of gleaming scalp.

"Madame," he said, "allow me to introduce myself. I'm Daniel Brokaw. I . . . represent Sister Angela."

"Pleased to meet you, Mr. Brokaw," Jessie said. She looped the reins around the saddlehorn, loose enough that the bay could drop his head to graze on the short, beaten-down grass by the pavilion, dismounted and walked toward the small brown man. "I'm Jessie Starbuck. I came to talk to the sister."

"And might I be so bold as to inquire your business with Sister Angela, Miss Starbuck?"

"Sure," she said. "I came to find out why her bully boys dismantled my saloon over in Center City, and beat one of my bartenders to death yesterday."

A flicker passed over Brokaw's features. "I'm sorry, Miss Starbuck, truly I am. Sister Angela is engaged in an undertaking of stupendous proportions, and sadly lacks the time to engage in conversation with casual visitors, even ones as undoubtedly charming as yourself. More to the point, she certainly has no knowledge of events such as you allude to."

21

"You mean to tell me your people don't bust up drinking establishments?"

"By no means. Sister Angela and her sledgehammer are famous for the damage they have wreaked in the Devil's dens called saloons, all across this fair state and in parts of Nebraska and Missouri as well. But as for violence to persons, permit me to assure you, neither the sister nor any of her numerous flock would ever countenance such acts."

Jessie planted herself right in front of him, hands on hips, so that his nose was practically pressed between her generous breasts. "Listen, Mr. Brokaw," she said, "I can go around you, or I can go over you. If you got such a distaste for violence to persons, I'd advise you to step aside."

He started to puff up like an angry toad. "Dan?" a feminine voice called from within the big tent. "Dan, is there something going on?"

"Nothing untoward, Sister Angela," he said over his shoulder. "A minor disturbance, nothing more. I'm dealing with it."

The flap opened. Jessie was not by nature an envious or a jealous person. But she could not help observing with a twinge that the evangelist who emerged blinking huge cornflower-blue eyes into the noonday sun was taller, blonder, and prettier than she. She wore a simple dress of brown gingham, like any local farm girl. She filled it out considerably better than most, though.

"Hello," she said at sight of Jessie. "I'm Sister Angela."

Jessie unset her jaw. "I'm Jessie Starbuck. I own the Liberty Saloon in Center City."

The big blue eyes grew wider. "And you're here to see me? I must say this comes as something of a surprise, Miss Starbuck."

"I said I was taking care of it," Brokaw said aggrievedly.

She brushed his cheek with her fingertips. "Dear Dan. Always so solicitous of me." She looked back at Jessie. "You came to see me, Miss Starbuck; here I am. If you care to step inside, we can talk. I find the sun has a most dreadful effect upon my complexion."

22

She held the flap open. Jessie ducked inside. Brokaw made as if to follow.

"If you'd be so kind as to excuse us, Dan," the evangelist said.

A muscle in the side of Brokaw's lantern jaw worked. Then he nodded and turned away.

Sister Angela let the flap fall. It cut off the blinding invasion from outside like the blow of an axe.

Jessie blinked around. She seemed to be in a sort of antechamber, divided from the rest of the pavilion with walls of fabric. The tent's interior had been dim, after the glare of outside; now the gloom seemed cavernous. As her eyes adjusted, she noticed the little room was furnished like somebody's parlor, with overstuffed chairs with antimacassars on the backs and a flowered rug on the floor.

"You'll have to forgive poor Dan," Sister Angela said. "Before salvation called his name he was a noted attorney and political reformer in Kansas City."

"He must have had his work cut out for him."

The evangelist smiled. "I do believe the Sisyphus-like nature of his task is what drove him into the arms of the Lord," she said. "Will you take a seat?"

Sisyphus-like? Jessie thought. *Where did this blond fluff learn to talk like that?* Warily, she perched on an off-white chair cushion with dogwood blossoms embroidered on it. Sister Angela sat down across from her.

"May I have you served tea, or cool refreshing water?"

"No, thank you," Jessie said. "There's something I need to talk to you about."

"Very well," the evangelist said with a smile. "What business brings you here, Miss Starbuck? I suppose it's too much to hope that you've come here in the throes of repentance, seeking your soul's salvation?"

"That it is," Jessie said grimly. Sparing no details, she described her arrival in Center City the day before. When she described the fate of the bartender Bryce, Sister Angela gasped, rose to her feet, and turned away.

23

Because it was much darker inside than out, it had initially seemed cooler as well. That illusion was wearing off. It was starting to feel stuffy. Parlors of the day were *supposed* to feel stuffy, but at least they had windows. This was overdoing it, to Jessie's way of thinking.

Sister Angela waved a hand at her without turning. "I'm sorry for the interruption," she said. "I have a highly sensitive nature, and what you told me was most disturbing to it. Pray continue."

Since the evangelist's back was turned Jessie felt free to let her skeptical frown show as she finished telling of her intervention and Police Chief Coates's inaction. By the time she was done, Sister Angela had turned around to face her.

"Are you familiar with my work, Miss Starbuck?" she asked quietly, sitting on the arm of the chair she had occupied.

"Not before yesterday."

"Are you certain you have never heard of me? The good Lord has blessed my crusade with some small notoriety in the nation's press. I have it on good authority that steel engravings of myself and Ezekiel have been reproduced as far away as the Alaskan Territories and the Sandwich Islands, to the dismay of the booze interests."

" 'Ezekiel?' "

The blond head nodded. "My sledgehammer, of course. My inseparable companion when I go personally on my missions of redemption."

"When you go and intimidate folks and destroy their property, you mean."

"Precisely." She put hands on her thighs and leaned forward, eyes aglow. "Now, you may wonder how I come to name my mighty hammer Ezekiel. Well I'll tell you. Ever since I was a little girl, reading of the prophet Ezekiel's vision of the fiery wheel has filled me with the spirit. Now, since I—"

"Pardon me for interrupting," Jessie said, "but I came to discuss a cold-blooded murder."

24

Sister Angela gasped, then nodded. "I can certainly see how your mind would be fixed on such morbid and distressing events, Miss Starbuck. But I must assure you, neither I nor any of my faithful had anything to do with them."

"You've admitted yourself you make a practice of destroying saloons."

"That's *things,* Miss Starbuck. Things have no souls; people do. My business is saving those souls from themselves. My mission and my message are Love. The Divine Love which fills my soul to overflowing, which makes my heart cry out for sadness at the thought of all those poor wretches out there groaning in their servitude to the Demon Rum."

"My employees said the mob came from your Temperance Army," Jessie said flatly.

Smiling angelically, Sister Angela shook her head. "One cannot give much credence to the testimony of low sorts such as find employment in the boozeries. You are obviously a woman of quality and discernment, Miss Starbuck; I can only believe that your acquaintance with such types has been scant."

She folded her hands in her lap. "No doubt the frightful events were actually the work of patrons maddened by drink."

There had been precious few occasions in Jessie's life when she found herself without a word to say. This was one of those times.

Finally she stood up. "I'm not sure we're even speaking the same language, Sister Angela," she said. "But I hope you'll understand this: I'm not closing the Liberty. And I'm not letting *you* close it. Good afternoon."

Sadly the evangelist shook her head. "You have a fine, clear spirit," she said. "Such a pity that Satan has clouded your eyes. Clearly, it is because you permit your brain to dominate your heart."

She rose, held out her hands. "Will you not bend your

knee and pray with me? We can together beseech the Lord to save you. It's not too late."

Jessie turned and stormed from the pavilion.

Her mind a seethe of wordless outrage, Jessie gave the bay his head on the ride back. He was a splendid mount; Alex Starbuck had raised his only child to be a consummate judge of horseflesh. Gruff, bearded Bern McAllister, who had lost an arm to a Yankton Sioux Minié ball during the Minnesota uprising of 1862, had a handsome string in his stable.

The shadows were lengthening when she judged she was four miles from Center City. She reined the gelding to a walk. He was blown, his sides pumping in and out like bellows. *Maybe I should've gone a little easier,* she thought. She cast around for a place for him to get a drink of water, but saw nothing.

Halting the bay, she dismounted, poured water from her canteen into her palm, and let him lap thirstily at it. "There you go, boy," she murmured. "I know it's not much, but it'll wet your throat. We don't have too much farther to go."

That overstuffed blond slattern, she thought as the gelding's warm rough tongue rasped her palm. *Is she a sharper, or is she just dumb as a stone fencepost?* Jessie took justified pride in her ability to read people. But she found the evangelist a blank brick wall.

The bay bobbed his head with renewed energy. For a moment she figured he must have managed to suck up more water than she thought. Then he lifted his face and shrilled a neigh of greeting.

She turned and looked back the way she had come. Less than a quarter mile away four riders were following her track, coming at a gallop.

Even at this distance, she could see they had bandannas tied over their faces.

★

Chapter 4

Quickly she tied the canteen back to the saddle's front rigging rings and mounted. The bay seemed to sag beneath her. Leaning forward almost onto his neck she spurred him into a run.

Most likely the four had followed her from the Temperance Army camp. Or maybe they were just highway robbers who had spotted a lone female rider and marked her as easy prey—though Jessie hadn't been brought up to believe in coincidence.

Either way, their mounts were fresher than hers.

The bay gave it his all, running with his neck stretched out and his head down, foam flying from his mouth. But they gained on her inexorably. Within a mile they had run her down.

"Where ya goin' in such a hurry, sweet thang?" laughed a lanky rider with a red bandanna over his face as he drew alongside her on a chestnut mare. He grabbed at her reins. "Why'n't you slow down and be *sociable?*"

Moving the reins to her left hand, Jessie slipped her right boot from the stirrup and straightened her leg. Her

27

right hand dove into the specially reinforced pocket on that side, came out with her custom-made .38 derringer. As the red-masked rider leaned toward her she brought it up, shoved it into his face, and fired.

Pink mist sprayed out behind his head. He pitched from the saddle without a sound. The buckskin following screamed in alarm and hopped to the side to avoid the body rolling over and over on the grassy ground. Its rider cursed and fought to control it.

Before she could turn, Jessie's right arm was seized from the side. A strong hand hauled her bodily out of her saddle. She fell against the heaving side of a big Roman-nosed pinto.

For a few thundering moments she was dragged like that, with her boot-heels scraping and bouncing along the ground and her gun-arm feeling as if it was being pulled out of the socket. Then the man on the pinto yanked back on the reins, bringing the animal to a rearing, eye-rolling stop.

Gasping for breath, her blond hair falling in her eyes, Jessie fought to get her feet under her. She felt the little silver derringer twisted from her grasp. She tried to remember what Ki had told her about escaping from grabs. Nothing really seemed to apply to this situation.

Another chestnut came booming up behind her. A little bandy-legged cowboy jumped down from the saddle and caught her in a bear hug.

"I got her!" he shouted. "Hoo, she's a pure she-devil, ain't she?"

About that time Jessie got her free elbow up and around and down in a strike that caught the brim of his hat on the way to his face. He yowled and reeled back. His hat fell off. His hair was brick red.

Her right arm was yanked cruelly up. The third rider appeared from somewhere, caught her around the waist, and lifted her off the ground. She kicked wildly at the air and tried to smash her head back into his face. He cannily kept his head ducked down behind one of her shoulders.

The man on the pinto let go of her wrist. "See if you c'n

hang onto her while I get down from here, Purdy."

"I got her!" the man who held her sang out. "Bitch kilt Wesley!"

The redhead had recovered. He was clutching at her legs, laughing. "Hoo, missy! Why you goin' and fightin' like that? We just wants to *fun* ya some!"

The man who had ridden the pinto had a big belly and blazing dark eyes. He came around to help the redhead seize her thrashing legs. Then the three of them lowered her to the ground.

I should have listened to Ki, she thought bitterly as the big-bellied man sat on her shins, pinning her legs to the black earth. The redhead scaled her like a monkey.

"Lessee what you're packin' under here," he said, straddling her belly. He reached down and ripped open the front of her shirt, baring her breasts. They were large, satiny-skinned and pink-nippled.

"Hoo!" he crowed in delight. "We got us a reg'lar banquet here!"

He grabbed her breasts, began to knead them like wads of dough. She spat at him. He giggled.

"Hey, now, Shorty," the big-bellied man on her legs said, "aren't you getting a bit ahead of yourself? We got us a little matter of *precedence* to discuss here—"

He was yanked suddenly backward off Jessie's legs.

Without pausing to look for a cause to the big-bellied man's departure, Jessie jackknifed instantly at the waist. Her long, strong legs wrapped themselves around Shorty's neck. With a heave of her hips she threw the little bare-headed cowpoke off her. Then she kicked blindly back over her shoulder.

The tip of her boot connected with something. With a grunt, the man who had ridden the buckskin released his grasp. She squirmed free, rolled, came up into a kneeling position.

She saw the big-bellied man squaring off against an opponent his own height—six feet or a hair over— and considerably slimmer. The newcomer had classically handsome features that looked as if they might have been carved from ice, and blond hair cropped to a silvery plush. He wore tan trousers, a white shirt, and a string tie. His head was ducked down behind his upraised fist, and he danced on the balls of his feet with the lightness of a trained boxer. His perfect lips were set in a half-smile of concentration.

"I'll fix you, you interfering son of a bitch!" the big-bellied man roared. He lunged forward, heaving a hamhock-sized fist roundhouse at the newcomer's head. The blond man ducked the ponderous but powerful blow, drove his fists left-right into the bulkier man's belly. The man's breath whoofed out of him, and he bent double.

From the corner of her eye Jessie saw red-haired Shorty flying at her. She turned to meet him, but before he reached her a black-clad leg whipped out, caught him in the gut, and threw him rolling into the grass.

Jessie turned. An immensely tall man loomed over her. He had a deeply tanned face, a powerful jaw framed by curly black sideburns. He smiled down at her, nodded politely.

Arms wrapped him from behind. "Get him, Shorty! I got him!" hollered the man who'd ridden the buckskin.

Shorty picked himself up and started forward, cocking a fist. The curly-haired interloper hauled both his feet off the ground and kicked the redheaded cowboy flying. Then he whipped his head back on his powerful neck.

It collided with the face of the man holding him with a loud crack. The rider screamed and staggered back clutching his face. Blood dripped from beneath the bandanna.

Jessie turned back to see the blond young man lean back away from another wild punch. Then he leaned forward into his opponent with an overhand right to the side of the jaw. The big-bellied man reeled backward three steps and sat down heavily.

The big curly-haired man was advancing on the rider whose nose he had broken. The man raised his hands in a poor imitation of a boxer. The curly-haired man grinned hugely. His right leg came whipping up and his

30

instep slapped the rider lightly on his blood-soaked cheek. Blinking surprise, the man brought his hands whipping up in a belated block.

The interloper had bent his leg at the knee without dropping it to the grass. Now he snapped it out in a kick to the pit of the masked man's stomach. The rider bent over, gagging. The curly-haired man planted his right leg and swung the left up in a savage straight-legged kick. It caught the rider midsection and hurled him to the ground.

"LeClerc!" the blond man shouted. "Vorsicht!"

The tall curly-haired man spun. Shorty was rising up from the ground hauling a big old Walker Colt bored-out and converted to take cartridges from a holster as long as his thigh.

The tall man took a long-legged dance step toward the red-haired outlaw and pirouetted. As the Walker came free, his right leg whipped out and around in a spinning kick that knocked the big six-gun flying out of Shorty's hand. The curly-haired man dropped his right foot to the ground and, using the momentum of his same spin, brought his left around in a scything arc that slammed against the side of Shorty's jaw. The little rider did a half-somersault, half-spin away from him, landed on all fours, and began scrabbling away.

The tall man laughed. It sounded like thunder rumbling up from deep in his huge chest. He started after the little red-haired man.

"No," the blond young man said. His voice was the voice of a man accustomed to being obeyed. The larger man stopped. "Let him go."

Jessie saw that the other two riders had already found their horses and were scrambling into the saddle. The big-bellied man slapped his pinto's fanny and sent him into a run while he was still hanging off the animal's side with a hand on the pommel and his foot in the stirrup.

Jessie looked back at the handsome blond man. He was studiously looking away from her.

"I trust the Fräulein has not been harmed by her ordeal,"

he said in excellent but distinctly accented English.

She looked down at herself. Her large breasts swung free in the warm afternoon air, sheened with a light coat of sweat. "Oh," she said.

She clutched the front of her violated shirt together in one fist, covering herself, and cast about for her hat. It had been knocked loose in the fracas, despite the string. She found it a few feet away, picked it up, drew a long hatpin from the band, and pinned her shirt shut. Then she turned to face her rescuers.

"I'm Jessie Starbuck," she said. "Thank you."

The blond man clicked his heels and bowed. The way he smiled as he did so kept him from appearing too mechanical or comic-opera. Now that the heat of battle was past, she realized he looked painfully young, eighteen or nineteen perhaps.

"I am Joachim Heinrich Jürgen Maria, Freiherr von Trott zu Pappenheim," he said. "It is an honor to come to the aid of a lady in distress . . . particularly when the lady in question happens to be the famous Jessica Starbuck."

"The pleasure's definitely mine, Baron," she said.

He raised a blond eyebrow. "You understand German?"

"A little. I'm familiar with the titles." She nodded at the baron's tall, dark shadow. "Who's your friend there with the fancy feet?"

"Ah, that is LeClerc, my man. He is a master of the arcane French art of *savate*—which, as you have gathered, entails fighting with the feet."

LeClerc finished helping his master on with his coat, handed him his hat, and bowed, less stiffly than the baron. "Enchanté," he said in a French Canadian accent.

Jessie was looking around for her little sneaky-pistol, spotted a silver gleam in a clump of grass, and walked over to retrieve it. Giving it a quick once-over, she decided it hadn't been damaged. She broke it open, dropped out the spent shell, slid another cartridge from her pocket into the chamber, and snapped the tiny weapon shut.

"I'm not one to look a gift-horse in the mouth, Baron," she

said, tucking the derringer back in its leather-lined pocket, "but recent events have put me in kind of a suspicious frame of mind. Just how is it that you happened to be passing this way when those owlhoots set on me? And how come you seemed to know who I was right away?"

Pappenheim smiled. "A gentleman will forgive a lady almost anything," he said, "especially one as lovely as yourself. And besides, you display a most laudable prudence. The explanation is simplicity itself: I am touring this splendid and barbaric land of yours. My loyal servant and I were passing through Center City on our way to observe the remarkable phenomenon of this Divine Love Temperance Army I have read so much about, when I chanced to learn that the noted female business magnate Jessica Starbuck was in the vicinity. It has long been my ambition to meet you, Fräulein Starbuck, so we rode instantly ahead in hopes of encountering you."

He held out an immaculately manicured hand palm-up. "Of course, it was hardly my wish to find you in such distressing circumstances. Nevertheless, it is my honor to have been of service."

"That you were, Freiherr," she said. "That you were."

Her bay was grazing contentedly not fifty yards away. That was a pleasant surprise; most horses would've put their heads down and rushed straight on back to the barn in terror. She walked back along the track she had ridden to where the man she had shot lay face down in the grass.

Fat black flies buzzed all around. A glimpse at the back of his head—a sizable chunk of which was missing—told her all she needed to know.

"Tarnation," she said. "I wanted to ask who sent these yahoos after me."

"Fräulein Starbuck," the baron said from behind her, "surely a person in your position is liable to attract numerous enemies. If I could learn that you would be riding this trail this afternoon, other, less well-intentioned parties could have as well."

She sighed, nodded. *Guess I have attracted kind of a*

passel of enemies, she thought. *Though I have an idea that the party who sent these back-shooters was female, blond, and too top-heavy for her own good.*

"Would the Fräulein do me the honor of permitting myself and my man to accompany her back to Center City?" Pappenheim asked.

She pushed a sweat-lank strand of hair from her eyes and grinned. "Sure," she said, "and thank you kindly. And call me Jessie."

"Gladly," the baron said with a bow, "if you will consent to call me Joachim."

"Deal."

The ride back to Center City passed quickly. LeClerc didn't have much to say, but the dashing young baron—mounted on a high-stepping black stallion with a white star and one white stocking—more than took up the slack. He was a charming traveling companion, quick-witted and amusing. He kept Jessie laughing with tales of his adventures, from Prussia to Paris to the wilds of the American West.

He was not, she had decided, nearly as young as he looked. She had just about decided that that was a good thing when they reined-up in front of the Liberty.

The street was filling with shadow. Jessie swung down from the bay, trying not to grimace as she did so. Raised on horseback, she wasn't prone to getting saddle sore—but she had taken a good crack on the tailbone during her fight with the masked men, and her whole backside ached.

"Joachim," she said, looping the reins over the hitching rack, "I'd be honored if you and Monsieur LeClerc would join me for supper."

He reached a gloved hand down. She hesitated, then placed hers in it.

"I much regret," he said, bending from the saddle to kiss her hand, "that pressing engagements do not leave me the option of accepting your gracious invitation."

He straightened. "If I may presume, though, I certainly hope that I may enjoy your company again soon."

"Yeah," Jessie said, a little hollowly, "sure." She heard the double doors whisper open at her back, sensed a familiar presence. She didn't turn.

The baron tipped his hat. "Good afternoon, Fräulein." He and LeClerc turned their horses around and rode south through the gathering dusk.

She watched them to the end of the block, then turned and swept past Ki into the saloon. Inside it was dark.

"Good grief, can't we get some *light* in here?" she demanded in a strident voice. "Has everybody gone to sleep?"

"Everyone is resting," said Ki, coming in after her. "They have spent a hard day working to repair the damage to your establishment."

She looked at him sharply, opened her mouth to say something brisk. Then she made a face and shook her head.

"You're right, Ki," she said. "I hadn't ought to go snapping at the help like that. Don't know what got into me."

"You are unaccustomed," he said placidly, "to having men ride away and leave you standing in the dust."

She glared at him. "I hate it when you're right," she said. "Now get out of my way. I'm dying for a bath."

★

Chapter 5

The women standing on the covered wooden walk in front of Cubbins' General Store on the town square turned their heads to look disapprovingly as Jessie and Ki walked past.

"—no better than she *has* to be," she heard one say.

"I hear tell she's heiress to an *amazing* fortune," said a second. "And look at her, gallivanting around town dressed like a common saddle-tramp."

"What do you expect," a third said piously, "from a so-called *lady* who would stoop to running a *saloon*?"

Dressed in her customary cowhand garb, Jessie felt the muscles of her back tighten and her fists clench. "The warrior ignores the idle cackling of hens," Ki said.

She gave him a fierce sideways look. "One of these days I'm going to get fed up with those aphorisms of yours."

"Nonsense," he said. "They only perturb you because you know they're right."

She scowled at him a beat longer, then laughed. "The good people of Center City may not like us," she said, "but I notice they don't decline to drink at my establishment." The Liberty had reopened the night Jessie returned from her unproductive visit to Sister Angela, and had been doing increasingly brisk business in the two days intervening.

It was a little after eleven. The sun blazed forth from a cloudless sky, and the heat was already stifling. Jessie had risen about ten, bathed, and breakfasted. That was one thing about saloon keeping that she decided she liked; though she was accustomed to ranchhand's hours—rising with the sun and going to bed not long after it did—she was not by nature an early riser. Working and rising late appealed to her.

Ki, of course, had been up since some God-awful hour, practicing the *kata*—prearranged combat patterns—of his martial art *te*. The man seemed to function flawlessly on almost no sleep. Jessie envied him the capacity.

They walked away from the square. They had no set destination in mind. She felt the need to stretch her legs. Ki, as always unless ordered otherwise, stuck with her.

"Words and actions are not always in accord," Ki said.

"You're doing it again."

"It is my nature, as—" He glanced at her. Her pretty face was beginning to cloud up like a thunderstorm brewing. He cut himself off.

Then she clutched his arm as a chair came crashing through a plate glass window half a block ahead.

They looked at each other. "Sister Angela?" Jessie asked. She felt as if she had thrown the gauntlet down on her visit to the Temperance Army, and had been expecting the buxom blond crusader to start making moves in her direction soon.

Ki shrugged. Jessie took off down the street toward the sound of angry voices spilling out of the busted window.

The sign on the building's false-front read, THE FREEMAN. Lying on the boardwalk amid shards of broken glass was a printed placard reading, "D. COULTER, JOB PRINTER." The door was open. Ignoring Ki's warning cry, Jessie marched inside.

A half-dozen men, some of whom Jessie recognized as locals, were rampaging through a small office, scattering papers and trying without much success to kick an overturned

37

desk to pieces. A tall, slender young man with longish blond hair stood blocking the doorway to the back. He wore an ink-stained printer's apron over white shirt and brown trousers.

"Gentlemen, please," he was saying. "This country was founded on the principle of freedom of the press—"

"Free thinker!" A burly mechanic aimed a roundhouse punch at the blond man's thin, aristocratic nose. The printer ducked. The big grimy-nailed fist struck the doorjamb with a loud crack.

"Oow!" moaned the mechanic, clutching his fingers. "I busted my hand! Get him, boys!"

"Panderer!" another shouted.

"Sodomite!" added a third. He was a wiry man with a sunburned neck. For good measure he sent a straight left punch flying toward the printer's face.

The printer weaved aside. "While I defend the right of everybody to live as he chooses," he said, "honesty compels me to resist your imputation, sir. Whatever else I am, I am no sodomite."

"Yer promotin' the sins what got Sodom and Gomorrah destroyed by a wrathful God!" the man with the sunburned neck declared. He drove his fist at the printer's midriff. The aproned man stepped aside.

"Just what in the name of Heaven is going on here?" Jessie demanded.

Heads turned to look. "This here varmint," said a rangy specimen with a squint, "is corrupting the morals of our young people with the filth he prints."

"We're concerned citizens of this fair city, come to bust up his press," said a fat man whose beard was streaked with the remnants of today's breakfast, if not from the whole week's.

"We come to bust *him* up!" a gap-toothed man added.

"He's a God-damned sodomite!" the sunburned man declared.

"So all six of you are breaking up his shop and trying to thrash him," Jessie said. "My, that's brave."

"Now, missy," the tall squinty one said, "don't go stickin' your ladylike nose in where it don't belong."

"I know her," the mechanic with the injured paw exclaimed. "She's the fancy-britches from outta town, come into run the saloon. She ain't no lady."

"I am indeed a lady," Jessie, "but you're clearly no gentleman. You're a yellow mongrel who has to run with a pack to find his courage."

"Why, you—" He reached his good hand to shove her.

She felt the presence of Ki, right behind her. Having taken her stand, though, she was damned if she was going to hide behind her bodyguard. Besides, he had taught her well.

She grabbed the extended hand by the little finger, sidestepped, bent the finger back toward the wrist. The mechanic howled and dropped to his knees.

"Your manners are as deficient as your bravery, sir," she said, and booted him smartly in the crotch.

The enthusiastic little man with the sunburn lunged at Jessie. Quick as a thought, Ki flowed between them. He brought the sunburned man up short with a sharp vertical backfist to the face, then front-kicked him in the chest and sent him sprawling back against his buddies.

They responded by shoving him heartily back at Ki. Ki grabbed a sleeve of one outflung arm, pivoted into the man, dropped to one knee, and hurled him gracefully over one shoulder out the window into the street.

The gap-toothed man took advantage of Ki's turned back to charge. From hands and one knee Ki launched a back-kick straight into the man's midsection. It picked him off the ground and threw him bodily back against the wall with a bang. He slid to the floor and curled around himself, gasping for breath.

The mechanic was on his knees clutching himself. Jessie kicked him in the jaw with the point of her boot. He measured his length on the floorboards and lay on his back, stunned. She stepped on his crotch again, hard, just to give him something to think about when he came back to his senses.

She looked at Ki. The fat man had caught him from behind in a bear hug. The squint-eyed man was closing in on him. She saw no need to intervene. Ki had the hooligans right where he wanted them.

A hand grabbed her right shoulder, rudely spun her around. She turned into it, knocked the hand away with her right fist. But she caught the heel of her right boot on the fallen mechanic's elbow, had to fight for balance.

The sixth man had on a bright red flannel shirt with the tails out. He grinned, cocked his big grimy right fist, and launched it straight for Jessie's face.

A hand caught it in mid-flight. "That's no way to treat a woman," the shop's proprietor said mildly.

"You keep out of this, you panderin' anarchist bastard!" the man in the red shirt roared. He yanked his fist free, drew it back to smash the printer in the face.

Jessie brought her right boot up and around in a swift roundhouse kick to the solar plexus. The breath oofed out of the red-shirted man. He doubled over.

Before he recovered, Ki materialized behind him to drop an elbow smash into his kidneys. The man dropped to his knees, gasping in pain. Ki grabbed him by the collar, twisted it taut around his dirty neck, hauled him to his feet, and gave him the bum's rush, sending him wobble-legging out the door to join his buddies groaning in the street.

"Are you all right, Miss?" the printer asked.

"Couldn't be better," she said, grinning. Up close he wasn't as young as she'd thought at first, early thirties maybe. He was definitely presentable, with big blue eyes behind the square lenses of his spectacles. Too bad he wasn't more of a fighter.

"I'm Jessie Starbuck," she said. "And this is Ki, my bodyguard." She stuck out her hand.

After a moment's hesitation the printer took her hand and shook it firmly. "Pleased to meet you, Miss Starbuck. I'm David Coulter." He shook hands with Ki. "Thanks for lending a hand."

"You are fortunate we happened by when we did," Ki

40

said. "You did not offer much resistance to the destruction of your premises."

Coulter shrugged. "I find a man has little to gain from fighting with his neighbors," he said, "but I thank you for your help, once again."

"At least they didn't get through to your presses," Jessie said, giving her bodyguard a warning look. Diplomacy was not always the warrior's strong suit—he had a pretty flowery and Oriental way of doing it sometimes, but he tended to just bluntly speak his mind. Jessie didn't want to alienate the printer; they had few enough friends in this Godforsaken little town as it was.

Besides, he was kind of cute. Even if he wasn't her type.

Coulter smiled. "No. They haven't managed to do that yet." She looked inquisitively at him. "Oh, this is the third time a mob has broken in here. So far all they've done is minor damage."

He looked out the gaping front window at the street. The would-be mob members had made themselves good and scarce.

"Replacing that glass is getting to be kind of pricey, though."

"What do you do to arouse such antagonism, Mr. Coulter?" Jessie asked. As she did she frowned slightly. There was something vaguely familiar about that name.

"I publish a paper," Coulter said. "It's called *The Freeman*. Some of what it has to say is fairly controversial."

He stopped and picked up a little four-sheet newspaper with a bootprint across it, dusted it off, handed it to Jessie.

"A sample of my work. You can judge for yourself whether or not you regret having stopped those men from breaking up my presses."

" 'But some persons are in the habit of saying that the use of spiritous liquors is *the* great source of crime,' " Jessie read aloud, " 'that it "fills our prisons with criminals" and that this is reason enough for prohibiting the sale of them.

" 'Those who say this, if they talk seriously, talk blindly

41

and foolishly.'" She frowned and looked up at him. "Pretty heady stuff, Mr. Coulter, but I'm bound to say, nothing I don't agree with."

"It goes on to say that 'the greatest of all crimes are wars that are carried on by governments, to plunder, enslave, and destroy mankind.'"

She shrugged. "Did you write this?"

He shook his head. "No. Would that I had. It's from a broadsheet titled, *Vices Are Not Crimes,* by Lysander Spooner. That's his portrait on the wall."

Jessie turned to glance at the framed photograph next to the door to the shop proper. It was of an elderly party with flowing white hair and a truly magnificent beard.

"I reckoned that was your grandfather," she said.

Coulter laughed. "No indeed. Except, perhaps, spiritually. Mr. Spooner is the nation's foremost advocate of natural law and individualism. His essay, which I've undertaken to reprint in installments . . ." He tapped the sheet of newsprint with his fingernails. " . . . asserts that 'vices are those acts by which a man harms himself or his property,' whereas '*crimes* are those acts by which one man harms the person or property of another.' It's his contention that only real crimes—which harm another, not just oneself—are the only things which can in sense and justice be prohibited by law."

"Which I reckon is why those men were calling you by all those slanderous names, Mr. Coulter," Jessie said.

He nodded slowly. "Precisely."

"Well, I guess I can see how some low sorts might get riled up about such talk," she said.

"Not only those, I fear." He took off his glasses, polished them with a handkerchief. "You're the owner of the Liberty Saloon, are you not?"

"Yes, indeed, sir. As I guess you know, yours is not the only establishment hereabouts to have trouble with bands of ruffians."

"Indeed not. It was quite inexcusable what happened at the Liberty—and Chief Coates's inaction is less excusable still. I have been intending to run an editorial denouncing the violence done, and what our esteemed police chief has failed to do, in my next edition. In fact, it comes to me I've been quite remiss in failing to interview you before now on the tragic events in question."

He put his glasses back atop his long, thin nose. "I confess, I'm more of a pamphleteer than a journalist. May I offer you and Mr. Ki something to drink, Miss Starbuck?"

"Jessie, please. And yes, thank you."

He righted the office chair which had not been hurled through the window, and held it for Jessie, who sat. Then he ducked into the back room.

"Were you shocked by Mr. Spooner's editorializing?" she asked Ki.

He grunted. "The obsession you Americans have with denying one another such pleasures of life as drink, gambling, and sex never ceases to amaze me," he said. "In Japan, so long as one performs his duty, no one begrudges him such diversion."

"Ah, but in America we too often feel it's our *duty* to deny people such diversions, Mr. Ki," said Coulter, coming back through the door. He held a tray with a bottle of bourbon and three glasses. "Have you been to the Orient, then?"

"I was born in Japan."

"Were you? I spent some time in the Orient myself, but I never reached the Eight Islands. I'd love to talk with you about the country someday."

Ki nodded solemnly. Coulter poured drinks for the three of them.

"I take it," Jessie said, holding up her glass to let the backsplash sunlight off the street play in its depths, "that you don't have much sympathy with Sister Angela's crusade."

"No. As you might have already inferred from my paper, I'm afraid my views and hers don't correspond at all." He sipped. "Still, I must admit I find her rather a fascinating woman. She's not necessarily what she appears to be."

"Oh, really?" Jessie said. "And what does she appear to be to you, Mr. Coulter?"

43

"David, please. She appears, at a cursory glance, to be nothing but a brainless blond-haired bigot, to risk overplaying the hand of alliteration. And yet she's far from unintelligent, and indeed rather thoughtful."

"And how do you come by this intelligence, David?" For reasons she couldn't name, Jessie felt slightly disgruntled at the thought of the handsome young editor passing too much time in the evangelist's company.

"I've read her pamphlets. If you'd like I can dig them up and show them to you."

"Please."

The printer rooted around among the papers the small mob had strewn about the office. "Here we are," he said, straightening up holding a sheaf of thin pamphlets like a full house.

Then he adjusted his glasses and peered out the hole where his front window used to be. "What's this?" he said.

Jessie rose and looked out. Across the street a barefoot youth was nailing a placard to the wall of a warehouse. Even from here she could read the message printed on it in huge letters:

PRAISE THE LORD!
SISTER ANGELA'S
DIVINE LOVE TEMPERANCE ARMY
IS COMING TO
YOUR FAIR TOWN!

★

Chapter 6

The sounds of gaiety came thumping up through the floor of Jessie's room above the Liberty. She turned up the kerosene lantern beside her bed and picked up one of Sister Angela's pamphlets from a doily-covered table. She sat in a chair with her hair unbound and gleaming gold in the lantern's glow.

The first pamphlet was fronted by an engraved illustration of Sister Angela holding her trusty sledgehammer Ezekiel. It sported the lead-footed title "Despatching the Demon Rum Back to the Nether Regions," and chronicled the evangelist's adventures busting up saloons across Kansas, Nebraska, and Missouri. There wasn't much surprising to be found in it, though Jessie noted that Sister Angela made a great point of her efforts to avoid harming persons in the course of her work of destruction. It was every bit as talky as the name suggested.

"Let her come and try it here," she said, tossing the pamphlet onto the bed. "Just let her."

The second pamphlet made her blink. It was called "The Rights of Woman Vindicated." To Jessie's dismay

45

it made considerable sense. It was as floridly written as the first leaflet, but fairly well-reasoned, indicating that the voluptuous evangelist was not as dumb as she looked, at least to Jessie. Jessie couldn't find much faulty with the main tenet, which was that women were just as intelligent and capable as men.

The one place Sister Angela lost her was in her insistence that *temperance* was tied up with women's rights somehow. Angela seemed to believe that outlawing alcohol would preserve women from being beaten by drunken spouses. Jessie could never make herself believe booze "made" anybody do anything; if a man was of a sort to hit his wife while under the influence of strong drink, she reckoned, he'd find occasion to while sober, too, sooner or later. Her solution to a such a man involved a liberal application of double-ought buck to the breadbasket. She knew that a wife employing such drastic methods against her husband faced prison—and maybe changing that was a better target for a distaff crusader than enforcing temperance.

Jessie shook her head. The situation had seemed simpler when she could dismiss Sister Angela as a possibly malevolent piece of fluff. That the evangelist wasn't stupid could get to be inconvenient, if they happened to butt their blond heads together. As it seemed was fixing to happen.

That she was sincere bothered Jessie. *Here she's trying to make the world a better place, according to her lights,* she thought. *Seems unjust to be going up against her.*

Jessie had to take a deep breath and remind herself she wasn't the one forcing the issue. She tossed the remaining pamphlets on the bed and massaged her temples with her fingers. It was almost time to go back down and look in on the saloon again.

Here I am, she thought with a sour half-smile, *head of a worldwide business empire. And what am I doing? Spending my time running some penny-ante saloon in a half-horse town in Kansas.*

She shook her head, then caught herself by surprise with

46

a yawn. The saloon wasn't the point. It was merely the ground she had chosen to make a stand on.

And Starbucks weren't in the habit of taking too many backward steps.

Martin Cordwainer was drunk again, but his fingers didn't know it. He might have been a trained astronomer, and then again, he might not. But he did know how to play piano. He belted out lively tunes for the girls to swing their skirts and highstep to—not quite far enough to be improper—on the little stage with the limelights around it. And all the while he was swaying on his stool like a flagpole in a blue norther.

Ki stood to one side of the main room, a shadowed silent figure, unobtrusive but impossible to miss. The patrons were content to ignore him for the serious business of drinking. The first few nights the Liberty had been reopened there had been a few incidents—customers who couldn't hold their liquor, or who thought to take advantage of others who couldn't. In each case Ki's reaction had been swift and economical as a prairie rattler's strike. He hadn't hurt anybody—not in any lasting way, anyway. But the word had soon gotten out, and now the saloon's patrons were careful to mind their manners.

Ki drew no satisfaction from intimidating the locals. He was pleased to serve his employer honorably and well, in the small duties as well as the large ones. As for his triumphs over would-be brawlers, a warrior won no glory swatting horseflies.

He stood with arms folded, relaxed yet always ready. He did not focus attention on any part of the lantern-lit establishment, on individual customers; he allowed the totality of it to flow through his ears and eyes into his awareness, the dance of shadows, the tinkling of the rump-sprung upright piano, the mountain stream burble of conversation, the rhythms of revelry and drink and petty gambling. If anything disturbed those rhythms, he would know at once.

That left the greater part of his awareness free, to turn inward, to concentrate on Void and seek serenity without intention. Though he would never admit it to another—and barely to himself—thoughts of his golden-haired employer were intruding, as they so often did. And not just thoughts concerning her welfare.

In his mind he formed the image of a stone, a pebble white and smooth from the bottom of a stream, and then he closed his mind about it like a fist. Such thoughts could never be more than unwelcome distractions.

The piano tinkled at the outer reaches of his awareness. Dancing girls flaunted their skirts and layers of colorful ruffled petticoats. A voice raised, the legs of a chair squeaked back across plank flooring . . .

A man stood up, red-faced, cocking a fist. Ki was there, standing beside the table, not close enough to intrude, but close enough to intervene.

"May I help you, gentlemen?"

The eyes of the man who had risen flicked from the three who sat across from him to Ki. Ki looked at him with the flat black gaze of a statue. The man moistened his lips with a thick tongue.

"Ol' Charlie here don't cotton to losin'," said one of the men still seated.

Ki turned his eyes on them. "You are welcome to game here," he said in a voice pitched to carry to their ears, but no farther. "Your play is honest, of course."

The three looked at each other, then back in the general direction of Ki. Having once done so, none of them seemed to want to make contact with those black eyes again.

"Yep," the spokesman said, bobbing his head so vigorously the grizzled bristles on his thin cheeks made scraping sounds against the collar of his plaid flannel shirt.

Ki looked to the standing man. His prominent Adam's apple rode up and down his gullet, and he nodded.

"Reckon I let my temper git the better of me," he said. He didn't look Ki straight-on either.

48

Ki nodded slowly. "By all means continue, gentlemen," he said, "in the spirit of friendship."

A patter of quick assents, and the men settled back to their cards, with occasional nervous looks over shoulders. Ki glided back through the crowd to his station by the wall. This time he had little trouble focusing his being on nothingness.

"Mr. Ki?"

At the sound of the tentative female voice he stirred, came back to himself and his surroundings. It was the redheaded dancing girl, Charity Anne. A vague part of him had been aware of her approach. Sensing that she posed no threat, that segment of his mind had not broken him from his meditation.

Now he nodded, smiled slightly. "Miss House."

She smiled back, shyly. Her almost metallic hair was piled atop her head, with a curl falling daintily down beside either cheek. She wore a blouse cut low to emphasize ample breasts in a way that should have thoroughly scandalized the burghers of a God-fearing Kansas town. As yet, Ki had heard no complaints from the patrons, though.

Behind her he noted that the crowd had begun to thin out. Closing time approached. Cordwainer played slow mournful tunes on the battered old upright, swaying with drunken exaggeration to the rhythm, eyes shut tight.

"The way you always stand there," she said, "you're like—some kind of old statue, or something. Don't you ever get bored?"

He shook his head.

"I'm about finished up here for the night," she said. She glanced around, glanced back at Ki, dropped her eyes and bit her lips, very prettily.

"I live in a little house on the outskirts of town," she said. "Well, more like a shack, really. Anyway, people say the Temperance Army is on it's way here and going to arrive any day now, and with that and all the things that have been going on it's getting so I'm a mite afraid to walk by myself. I was wondering—would you be willing to escort me home?"

At the railing of the gallery looking down on the saloon from the upper floor, Ki saw Jessie appear. Her hair was piled any which way on top of her head, with little wisps hanging down here and there, and her eyes were slightly squinted. Evidently she had dozed off for a spell, then roused herself to check what was going on below. He noted that she wore the pistol her father had given her— a Colt double-action .38, in a heavy .44 frame—in its worn gunbelt at her hip.

"I know it's a lot to ask," Charity Anne said.

"Not at all," Ki said. "It would be my honor."

"Aren't you afraid?" Charity Anne asked as they made their way through the dark of Center City's northern outskirts. The waning moon hung like a lantern, high in a starshot sky; a lone cloud had flung a wispy arm across its face, as if for support. The air was heavy with the scent of early dew on tall grass. Bullfrogs trilled, their cries sounding thin and far away. Off in the slow moon-silvered roll of the land two rival bands of coyotes were debating territorial privilege.

"Afraid?" Ki asked.

He saw her nod. She had a threadbare Mexican-style mantilla draped over her bare shoulders. "Of Sister Angela and her Temperance Army. They already—already killed poor Mr. Bryce. Now they're all coming *here*. And they're sworn to shut down the Liberty forever!"

"What is to fear?" Ki asked. "Death comes to all of us, sooner or later."

The woman shuddered. "I wish I could see things that way. The way I see it, I'd like to put it off as long as possible."

She gave a brittle little laugh. "Not that my life has been such great shakes to date. But I'm not too eager to let go of it regardless."

"I cannot tell you not to fear," Ki said. "But Miss Starbuck and I will protect you as well as we can."

50

She started to laugh even louder, broke off and shook her head. "I'm sorry, Ki, really I am. It's just—there's hundreds and hundreds of them, and two of you. It's a little hard to see how you can really *protect* us from them."

He smiled slightly into the dark. "You might be surprised," he murmured. "Understand, it is unlikely we shall be attacked by all of them at once. That does not appear to be the way Sister Angela operates; if she did, the Governor would have been forced to call the state militia out against her long before this."

"But the mob that attacked us before—"

"Was miles away from Sister Angela's great tent. They could do their evil work without her being blamed."

He looked down at her. "I do not say it will be easy. Nor do I say it will be safe; but life never is, no matter what we imagine. Still, if you want out—"

She shook her head firmly. "No. If Miss Starbuck and you can stick it out, I guess I can. Besides . . ." She smiled up at him. "Watching you, I get the feeling the odds against us aren't half as bad as they look."

They walked a time in silence. Then Ki raised his head and inhaled deeply. "It's very beautiful out here," he said.

Lacking much by way of a path, they were picking their way overland. Charity Anne clung lightly to his arm for support. He moved across the dark irregular earth as smoothly as fog.

"I guess it is," she said, peering uncertainly at the ground as she picked her way along. "I just don't often think of it that way. I'm from Pittsburgh, back East. I grew up without seeing much sky to speak of—tall buildings, the smoke that always covers everything. My father . . ."

She broke off shuddered, shook her head. "Well, let's just say I left town in a hurry. I didn't have much money, nor any idea where I'd go. Growing up, I always heard how people looking to build a new life—people with pasts to leave behind—came West. So I did, too. This is how far my money brought me."

She waved a hand around at the night. "I haven't ever

got used to it, I guess. All this flat open land, all this sky—it, well, it *scares* me sometimes."

He stopped, placed his hard brown hand over the hand she had laid on his other arm, gave her a reassuring squeeze. "Then stop a moment," he said softly.

She stood beside him, with an air about her as if she poised on tiptoe, waiting. After a scatter of heartbeats she said, "What do we do now?" whispering without real reason.

"Just listen. Breathe. *Look.* Open yourself to the night."

She had turned to stand facing him. At his instruction she drew in an exaggerated breath, closed her eyes, and lowered her head. Moonlight gleamed on the curve of moist, slightly open lips as she breathed deliberately.

He stepped back away from her, to give her room and let the fragrant night air envelope her. For a time they stood that way, in silence.

A flutter of motion, a squeak pitched high to the verge of hearing. She tensed, fists clenched at the end of downstretched arms.

"What's that?" she cried. She didn't open her eyes.

"A bat," he said, as the tiny shadow flitted in circles about them, like a piece of the night brought to life.

"A bat!" she shrilled. She squeezed her eyes more tightly shut and seemed to hunker in on herself. "Ooh, get it away!"

His laugh was low and gentle. "He won't hurt you. He's out hunting insects. We're much too big for prey."

With a visible effort she forced some of the tension out of herself, allowed her head to raise. Her eyes were still closed, but not so fiercely.

"I've always been afraid of bats, since I was a little girl," she said in a small voice. "They're so—so creepy."

The creature was still orbiting them, getting their measure with its tiny cries. "They are nature's creatures. No more, no less."

The bat began to wing in closer. Charity Anne tensed again.

"He's only curious," Ki said. "He wonders what we are.

Wouldn't *you* be curious if you encountered a bat the size of a barn?"

She giggled, then held her head full up. The bat flew close. She flinched, once, as its wingtip brushed her cheek, but she held her ground.

The little animal circled her once more, then went its way into the black with its darting irregular flight.

Ki touched her on the arm. "There," he said. "You have faced your fears, and found them empty. You have a warrior's spirit."

She smiled, continued to stand, unspeaking. In time she raised her head slowly, opened her eyes. She looked past him—at the night, and the open darkened land, and the sky. And then she did look at him.

"It's *wonderful,*" she breathed. "Really, I never really *saw* it before. It was all so threatening and strange."

"Do you feel threatened now?"

She shook her head. Her eyes were half-shut; curved wedges of moonlight glittered on the whites, beneath the lowered lids. Her lips were parted.

He bent his head and kissed her.

Her body jolted, as if the contact shocked her. For a moment he wondered if he had overplayed his hand. It was a familiar risk; he was not white, and to be caught taking liberties with a white woman without her permission . . .

She opened her mouth to his. Her body flowed against his, flowed around him, molding to him and enfolding him like water.

Their tongues strove briefly together. Then she broke away, held him at half the extent of her arms and looked at him with shining eyes.

"I've never known anyone like you, Ki," she breathed. "You're so strong, and yet you don't go noising off about it. In some ways you're so private, it's like you're off on you're own little island. But some ways you're so *open.*"

She pressed herself against him once more. Raising her face, she licked once at his chin.

"I hope you don't think I'm a harlot," she breathed in

his ear. She ran a hand inside his shirt. It burned against his smooth skin. "It's just that—to be with a man I *want*, instead of one I have to be with . . ."

His arms went around her. He kissed her forehead. "Is it far to your house, Charity Anne?"

She giggled—a surprisingly girlish sound, almost enough to break the mood, but not quite. "It's a ways yet. I—I kind of took us the long way 'round." She snuggled against him and nibbled his throat. "I wanted to get more of a chance to get to *know* you."

"Perhaps we should move on, then," he said. He dropped one hand to knead her ass gently, to let her know he wasn't rejecting her. Her rump was nicely rounded, firmly muscled beneath his wiry fingers. "Your bed—"

She dropped to her knees before him, began to fumble with the buttons of his trousers. He stroked her dark shining hair until she popped him free.

She ran her tongue around the head of his half-erect member and smiled up at him. "You've opened me to the night," she said, low in her throat. "Why let it go to waste?"

Without waiting for an answer she took him in her mouth again. He moaned, softly, when the pleasure flowed from his groin and up and over him.

He took her head in his hands. His touch was gentle, but instantly she stopped and jerked away.

"Don't," she said, wiping at a trail of saliva that ran from her lips to the head of his sex. "Brings back . . . memories."

He drew his hands away. She smiled and went back to work.

She seemed to enjoy her work, and was expert at it. Her tongue teased around and around, drawing groans of pleasure from him; then she began to move her head back and forth, impaling her face upon him. Unlike many of the women Ki had encountered in this strange and often puritanical land, she knew not to use her teeth.

When she felt him commence to tense and quiver, she

clamped her lips firmly around his shaft, at the sensitive spot where it joined the head, and sucked till her cheeks went hollow. As his passion built his hands hovered in air to either side of her red-haired head. Unable to follow his instinctive desire to grab her he grabbed his own head, threw it back, and cried out hoarsely as he spent himself in heaving spasms. She did not pull away.

Only when she had milked him for all he was worth did she relinquish her oral grasp upon him. "I have to apologize for the slurping sounds I was making, there at the end," she said, carefully licking her lips clean. "Not very ladylike. Then again, what I was *doing* wasn't exactly ladylike either, so if you're not complaining about the one—"

She started to rise. He laid fingertips on her shoulder, held her on her knees.

"What are you doing?" he asked, a bit hoarsely.

She looked surprised. "Well I got a just a wee bit carried away. And now I figure, since you're done . . ."

"Lie down," he said firmly.

She blinked at him, then complied, easing down onto her back in the damp grass.

"Now pull your skirts up," he commanded.

With trembling fingers she obeyed. The skin of her thighs was dusted with freckles, and beneath them so pale as to seem almost greenish in the moonlight. The sparse hair of her sex was light-colored.

"What are *you* doing?" she asked, wide-eyed, as he knelt between her upraised knees.

He smiled. "Returning the favor," he said.

She squealed as he nipped the tender satin flesh of her leg, right behind the knee, and began to nibble his way downward.

★

Chapter 7

"Among the Eskimos of Greenland, you understand," the handsome young baron said as he poured pale wine, "it is the custom to bury small fowl for a period of some weeks before devouring them."

Jessie rested on her side on the blanket they had brought from town, propped comfortably on an elbow, watching the play of sunlight on the green bottle and the nearly colorless liquid. She wore her customary working garb of a man's blue shirt and jeans. There was no point in trying to maintain the appearance of a lady at this point; she could go around all the time dressed like a nun without causing the good people of Center City to revise their opinion of her one iota.

She wrinkled her nose. "Doesn't that make them . . . well, *gamy?*"

The baron laughed. "Indeed it does. But that is precisely the point, don't you see? They have no spices in such climes. The state the bird achieves after a few weeks is held to quite enhance the flavor."

He recorked the bottle, tucked it back in the picnic basket, held forth a stemmed glass from the Liberty, which kept a few such on hand among the more robust tumblers, mugs, and glasses, just in case. "Wine?"

"Please." She accepted the glass, sipped, and laughed. "And if you think you're going to put me off my feed with your stories of disgusting food, Baron, you've got another think coming. I'm famished—even if that chicken we packed is way short of being ripe by Eskimo standards!"

It was his turn to laugh. "You must forgive me, Jessica." Try as she might, she had not been able to convince him to call her "Jessie." "I have spent so much time among primitives and rustics on this extended Wanderjahr of mine that I have quite forgotten how properly to converse with a refined and civilized lady such as yourself."

Not as civilized as all that, she thought, eyeing the young nobleman over the rim of her glass. The tensions of bringing the Liberty back into business, facing the hostility of the Center City citizens, and waiting for the inevitable arrival of the Temperance Army, were whetting her appetite, and not just for the roast chicken and bread tucked into the basket.

It was pretty out here, on this little knoll overlooking the north fork of the Jericho. The gently rolling land was carpeted with wildflowers, white, blue, yellow, purple thistle. Butterflies whirled about like scraps of white and yellow silk caught in a dust devil.

The river—creek, actually—was about fifty feet wide here. It had risen a bit and begun to flow a little faster since Jessie and Ki had arrived, fed by fierce thunderstorms farther north. The thunderheads were piling up in the south, too. So far Center City had been spared, but the storms got closer every day.

Today was fine, though—fine enough that it was almost possible to ignore the hammering midday heat, and the constant Great Plains wind whispering in the long grass. Jessie's bay gelding and the baron's black stallion had their heads down and were contentedly grazing just over the crest of the hill. Their tails swatted lazily at horseflies that buzzed around, themselves too torpid with the heat to press their attacks.

The baron served them chicken, bread, and cucumbers from the basket. As they ate they swapped stories of their travels, the sights they had seen and the things they had done. Jessie downplayed the more hair-raising aspects of her adventures: no point in making it seem as if she were bragging, and intrepid as the youthful Prussian seemed, she didn't want to scare him off. For his part the baron refrained from telling any more stories of his unusual dining experiences.

As they ate they just naturally seemed to move in closer to one another—so they didn't have to reach so far to replenish their food and drink, of course. When they were full, she repacked the remains of the meal in the basket.

In the course of doing that, she wound up sitting next to Pappenheim. Their heads were close together. The sun was stinging hot on her skin. She could sense the firmly packed strength of him, smell the strong scented soap he had washed with that morning. His features were chiseled and perfect as those of a Greek statue.

Her lips parted. He tipped back his head, looked at her down his narrow nose, ice-blue eyes half-lidded, arrogant. Her mouth moved toward his . . .

One of the horses whickered. Nerves wound taut by anticipation, Jessie gasped, rolled quickly over. She wasn't wearing her revolver, thanks to Chief Coates's gun ban. As she moved, though, she was hiking up the right leg of her jeans, going for the two-shot derringer tucked inside the top of her boot.

David Coulter stood between the foot of the hill and the riverbank, blinking myopically up at them through his thick, square-lensed spectacles. The restless wind ruffled his longish blond hair.

"I'm terribly sorry," he called. "I didn't mean to intrude. It's just that I often like to go for a walk by the river, after lunch. I find it aids digestion."

"You're not intruding at all, Mr. Coulter," Jessie said.

58

"Matter of fact, the baron and I were just finishing lunch ourselves."

Pappenheim stood up behind her. She got up a little too quickly.

"Baron, this is David Coulter. He publishes a weekly newspaper, *The Freeman*. David, this is the Baron von Pappenheim. He's a Prussian. He's traveling around the world."

The baron clicked his heels and bowed. "I am honored to make your acquaintance, Herr Coulter."

"The honor's mine, Baron. Perhaps some time you can, ah, you can tell me of your travels."

"Perhaps it might sometime be arranged," the baron agreed in his crisp, precise accent.

Suddenly Coulter's pale blue eyes flicked past Jessie, and he seemed to draw in on himself. It reminded her of a panther gathering itself to spring, or a rattler coiling to strike. *That's silly,* she told herself. *Davey's a good boy, but he's harmless as a lamb.*

She turned to follow the publisher's eyes. A dark figure loomed from the crest of the hill behind them.

The baron turned to look as well. "All is in order, LeClerc," he said. "You may leave us."

The lantern-jawed French Canadian nodded and seemed to melt into the stuff of the hillside. Coulter watched him go with a thoughtful look.

"Well, it's good to see you, Miss Star—Jessie," Coulter said. "With your permission, I'll be about my business."

"Good-bye, David," Jessie said. "Nice to see you."

"Baron." The publisher nodded to the nobleman and walked on along the Jericho.

Pappenheim looked to Jessie. She brushed her hair back from her face. Whatever the mood had been before Coulter's appearance, it was gone now.

She wasn't sure whether she regretted that or not.

"I guess I'd better be getting back as well, Joachim," she said, brushing grass from the seat of her jeans. "Thank you for a lovely lunch."

The baron hesitated only momentarily before nodding with millimetric precision. "As you say, Jessie."

She knelt to finish gathering up the picnic things. She had her face down to hide her frown. "I didn't know we weren't alone, Joachim," she said without looking at him.

"You mean LeClerc, of course," Pappenheim said. "I thought it best to have him follow and keep an eye on us. You have a way of attracting trouble, dear lady."

She laughed. "Don't I know it," she said. "Still . . . I thought this was a private occasion, Baron."

He clicked his heels and bowed. "A thousand pardons, mademoiselle. I did what I thought best for you, as a man of noble birth is obliged to do. But assure yourself, we were as good as alone until that . . . young gentleman happened along."

She finished tucking the checkered cloth back over the leftover food and shut the basket. "I know you Europeans see manservants as not being the same thing as real people," she said, sitting back on her haunches and brushing away a wisp of unruly hair. "But I don't see things quite the same way. *Especially* under the circumstances."

He laughed. It was a good laugh, solid as the rap of his surprisingly scarred knuckles on oak. "Indeed, we were raised with different outlooks, Fräulein. But that is not what I meant. In accordance with my instructions, LeClerc kept himself at a good distance from us. He was not in a position to see anything that passed between us, nor hear anything pitched lower than a shout."

"I see." She rose. "But he turned up pretty quick when Da—Mr. Coulter arrived."

"LeClerc is the consummate bodyguard," the Baron said. "He has—how should one say it?—a particular sense, an instinct if you will, for when possible danger arises. He simply *felt* your Mr. Coulter's approach, and moved up to see if his assistance was required."

He looked at her for a moment with a slight smile. "Or perhaps this sounds far-fetched to you?"

"Not at all," she said, shaking her head. "My bodyguard, Ki has the same sense."

"Then we are both fortunate in our servants."

"Uh, yes," Jessie said. She had never thought of Ki as a servant, and was not about to start. But she had traveled enough with her father to know full well that people from different countries—even from different parts of her own country—had different ways of looking at things.

And just how do I think of Ki? she asked herself. It wasn't for the first time. And she wasn't going to waste a lot of time delving for an answer now.

She grinned at the baron. "Race you back to town."

"Certainly." He hesitated. "Though perhaps I should spot you a furlong—"

"In a pig's eye! Let's go!"

It started as a cloud of dust in the south, beyond the north fork of the Jericho.

Jessie and Ki first became aware of what was happening when a pack of local kids came pelting past the saloon down Central Avenue, Center City's main street, shouting, "Here they come!" They stepped out into the morning to gaze south at the tawny pillar rising against a horizon-distant bank of thunderheads into an otherwise immaculate blue sky.

"Sister Angela," Jessie said, half under her breath, "and her Temperance Army."

"So it begins," Ki said.

The double saloon doors swung open. Martin Cordwainer emerged into daylight, blinking blearily at the sun as if unsure what it was. Ki raised a brow; this was the first time he had seen the Liberty's piano player upright before noon.

Cordwainer raised a glass of red wine in one hand. "Ah," he said, "nothing so lovely as sunlight through wine."

He gestured at the dust cloud with his glass. "Lay on, fair combatants," he declaimed in a ringing voice, "and may the best woman win!"

61

Jessie jutted her chin, rolled it around. "Or the worse one," she murmured.

Ki frowned at her.

She jerked her head toward the doors. They slipped inside, where it seemed dark as a cave after the street's brightness.

"Such irresolution is unlike you," Ki said.

She sighed, shook her head. "I just don't know," she said. "Sister Angela is trying to make the world a better place. What am I doing here? This is . . ."

She waved a hand around at the tables, with the chairs upside down on them for cleaning, the fly-specked mirror, the bottles ranked on shelves behind the bar. "This is just a saloon. Is it really worth fighting for?"

"Your friend Mr. Coulter might say that the right of people to make choices for themselves is a thing worth fighting for," Ki said. "And that to deny people such choices is to treat them like property."

She glowered at him for a moment, then laughed. "Davey is a nice boy," she said. "Nice man. But I wouldn't think you'd pay too much mind to what someone like him says."

"It is not given to everyone to be a warrior."

From the street outside came a childish cry: "Yonder comes a carriage! *Here she comes!*"

Jessie glanced past Ki's broad shoulder, over the tops of the louvered swinging doors. A trap with a fringe top, riding high on its suspension and drawn by a dappled grey mare with blinders on, pulled to a stop in front of the Liberty. Wearing a yellow dress and wide matching hat, Sister Angela jumped lightly to the ground. Her driver, a barefoot, towheaded boy in overalls, handed her down a sledgehammer with a huge pink bow tied around it.

A farm wagon loaded down with Temperance Army faithful creaked to a halt behind the little lightweight carriage. The soldiers began to pile out. Sister Angela hefted Ezekiel, seemingly unfazed by its weight, turned toward the saloon, straightened her hat, and smiled.

"Sister Angela possesses commendable strength," Ki observed.

"Um," Jessie said. She turned and walked around behind the bar.

The doors swung inward, and in walked Sister Angela, cradling her fabled sledgehammer in both hands. With the ribbon tied under its head it looked like a giant lead lollipop. Behind her trooped a cluster of followers, including a sketch artist and two reporters with flying pencils from big city back-East papers.

The buxom blond crusader grounded the butt of the sledgehammer on the saloon floor with a thump. "Good morning, Miss Starbuck," she said in a clear, cheerful voice. "I reckon you know why I'm here."

Jessie faced her across the polished hardwood bar. "I reckon you know why *I'm* here, too," she said. "If you or your friends care to drink, that's fine. If you wish to sit and pass the time peaceably, you're welcome as long as you care to stay."

Sister Angela smiled and shook her head, making curls dance before her ears. "It is not to drink that I have come here," she said, "but to put a stop to drinking."

"You won't," Jessie said. "Try to molest any of my patrons or employees, or bust up the furnishings—"

She stepped out from behind the bar. In her hands she held a double-barreled shotgun, broken open. The brass bases of two waxed-paper cartridges protruded from the open breech.

"—and I'll put some blond hair on the wall," she said. For emphasis she snapped the weapon shut and clicked back the twin hammers with her thumb.

The gaggle of hangers-on recoiled with a gasp. One of the reporters backed clean against the Liberty's front wall. Only the honey-haired crusader stood unflinching, facing the huge double bores.

"I regret that you feel that way, Miss Starbuck," she said. "I am about the Lord's business, and He will not long be denied."

"When He comes here and tells me what I'm doing is wrong," Jessie said evenly, "then I'll call it a day. Now I

63

think you'd best leave. I feel a nervous tremor of my trigger finger coming on."

"Be careful," the evangelist said, "lest you be cast into the Lake of Fire."

She pivoted gracefully. As she did so her eyes swept across Ki, standing impassively and unobtrusively by, ready to thrust himself forward in case anyone offered harm to his employer. Not that that seemed any too likely, under the immediate circumstances.

Sister Angela stopped. Her morning-glory eyes widened, swept the half-Japanese warrior's rangy form up and down. Then she stalked out without another word, haughty and smooth as a grand duchess. Her followers went scrambling after.

"I thought you had begun to doubt what you were doing here," Ki said quietly, as the doors swung back and forth, giving off small animal squeaks as their arcs diminished.

Jessie eased in the hammers and dropped the shotgun's buttplate to the floor by her feet.

"What I'm doing now is getting my back up," she said. "I just don't take kindly to being pushed around by the likes of Sister Angela. No matter how holy she is."

★

Chapter 8

"*We* shall gather by the *wa*-ter," the crowd of women on Central was singing as David Coulter appeared in the swinging double doors of the Liberty.

Big round Andy was sweeping the floor of the saloon. "Oh, Mr. Coulter, hi!" he piped.

"Good morning, Andy."

The young man turned and headed for the back in a lumbering run. "Miss Jessie! Miss Jessie! Mr. Coulter's here!"

"I'll be right out," came Jessie's voice.

Andy came back. "She says she's coming, Mr. Coulter," Andy said.

"Thank you, Andy. How are you today?"

"I'm doing fine, thank you, Mr. Coulter." He turned and picked up a rag doll that was sitting on the bar. It had a stitched smile and black button eyes.

"Did you see what Miss Jessie gave me?" Andy asked. He held it out, eyes shining from his plump cheeks. "My bunny. Would you like to see her? I call her Daisy Bunny."

"Hello, Daisy." Coulter accepted the doll, cradled it,

65

inspected it thoroughly and gently. It had black button eyes and two nubs on its head vaguely reminiscent of rabbit ears.

He handed the toy back to Andy. "She's a very fine doll, Andy."

Andy beamed. "Miss Jessie is a very nice lady."

"So I gather, Andy," the publisher said. "So I gather."

"Do I hear my name being taken in vain?" Jessie said, emerging from the rear of the establishment.

"Not by us," David Coulter said, "though it's entirely possible the not-so-angelic chorus out there has ad-libbed it into a psalm or two."

He showed a grin that made him look twelve years old. "Not that it would likely be in any favorable context, I'm afraid."

Jessie laughed. "I'm not sure whether our friends out there are praying for my soul's salvation, or its consignment to perdition," she said.

"If it's any consolation, I'd say Sister Angela falls into the former category." He glanced back over his shoulder at the doors. "I'm not sure I can say the same for all of her followers, however."

Jessie sighed and shook her head. "That's the thing about so many people who call themselves Christian," she said. "They forget what Christ taught about love and forgiveness, and concentrate on how their enemies are going to Hell."

Andy hunched his head down and pressed his hands over his ears. "Oh, Miss Jessie. You're saying bad things now. I'm scared of the Devil, Miss Jessie."

"So am I, Andy," she said. "But I'm sorry; I didn't mean to scare you."

She smiled and touched his cheek. "Why don't you run along to the back, dear, and let me speak to Mr. Coulter. Please?"

"Sure, Miss Jessie. Reckon the pantry needs sweeping." He scooped up Daisy Bunny and waddled off.

"I fear the Devil," Jessie said, "but at the moment I'm more afraid of those who claim to do the Lord's work."

Coulter shrugged. "Disheartening, isn't it," he said, "how so often the best motivations seem to inspire people to do the worst things?"

"In the Eight Islands," said Ki, coming down the stairs from the second-floor gallery, "we seldom concern ourselves with matters of good and evil. Our motivations involve duty, loyalty—and ambition."

Coulter nodded, brow creasing thoughtfully. "And do you find that a better way, Mr. Ki?"

Ki thought a moment. "Just—different. Certainly, our way has produced its share of misery and hardship."

"Where have you been, Ki?" asked Jessie, who didn't have a lot of patience for ethical debates at the best of times.

"On the roof," her bodyguard answered, "observing."

"Anything out there look threatening?"

"Not immediately," Ki said, at about the time Jessie realized her question had been foolish. Had there been any apparent threats, Ki would either have stayed in place or immediately warned her on coming downstairs. "There are a few groups of young men roaming the streets. The only concentration of Temperance Army forces appears to be the women singing in front of this building."

Jessie couldn't restrain a smile at hearing the off-key corset chorus described as "forces." Ki viewed any potential danger to his employer, no matter how remote, in essentially military terms.

Then again, Sister Angela thought of the singing women in similar terms. They themselves probably did, too. They were part of an army, after all.

"So our songstresses came up with Sister Angela, too," Jessie said. "I didn't see anybody but males when I visited her camp outside Williams."

"Sister Angela makes a point of recruiting women—as you can see in those pamphlets I lent you, she considers herself to be fighting their fight," David Coulter said. "But a couple of them are our own local biddies, I'm afraid."

Jessie's lips drew back in a grimly thoughtful expression.

"You know the Center City citizens, Davey," she said. "How likely are they to throw in with this bunch?"

He shrugged. "As you and Mr. Ki know all too well, I'm almost as much of an outsider here as you," he said. "But I *have* been here longer, so I do know a little about how the good people of the town think. I don't think many people here have a stomach for real nastiness— such as what happened to your bartender Bryce—the fact that occasionally my editorials inspire them to bust up my shop notwithstanding. A bit of vandalism from the rowdy elements is one thing. Murder is another."

There was a crash, a thump, and an almost musical tinkling. All three turned to face the front of the saloon. Ki flowed instinctively into fighting stance between Jessie and the door.

A brick lay in a scatter of shattered glass, just inside where the front window had been.

"Unfortunately," David Coulter said, "Sister Angela seems to have brought plenty of ruffians with her who are capable of almost anything in service of their prophet."

The shouts and psalm-singing now came from far away. The tumult had a muted, indistinct, ominous quality to it, like the rumble of distant thunder—or the noise of battle.

From the roof of the Liberty, Jessie could actually see the bonfires in the Temperance Army camp right across the creek, flames dancing in the face of the night. They reminded her uncomfortably of the ceremonies that often preceded Indian attacks.

"Our esteemed chief of police denied Sister Angela permission to preach from the town square," Coulter said, standing beside her on the flat roof. "He wouldn't let them camp on this side of the Jericho's North Fork."

"I'm surprised he denied her anything her little heart desired," Jessie said bitterly. "He was ready enough to look the other way when her thugs beat poor Bryce to death in front of me."

"What Chief Coates wants above all is to have no trouble in his town," Coulter said.

"Wasn't it trouble when the mob wrecked the Liberty and killed Bryce? For that matter, how about the crowd that tried to bust up your print shop? Doesn't that count?"

"The chief has his own peculiar way of looking at things. He regards the Temperance Army, in his heart of hearts, as rather akin to a force of nature, like a flood or a tornado: something to be endured, to be contained if possible, but not something it's sensible to try resisting directly. He could not prevent the lesser mob from attacking your saloon, so his instinct was to try to hold down the repercussions, not make waves after the fact, when there was nothing, to his mind, to be accomplished."

"What about justice?" Jessie demanded.

Even in the darkness, lit only vaguely by the bucketsful of stars strewn overhead, Jessie could see the irony in his smile. "That's a bit too abstract a concept for a small-town chief of police to grasp, Jessie. Or at least, for Norman Coates."

Wisps of Sister Angela's voice came floating to them, like shreds of a trumpet fanfare blown on the wind. Jessie's ears could wring no sense from them. *Of course,* she thought, *I don't know if that'd be any different if I could hear her perfectly.*

"Our evangelical friend is blessed with a remarkable set of lungs," Coulter remarked.

Jessie looked at him pretty sharply sidelong, unsure whether he was making a sly reference to the frontage of her person, which was even more impressive than Jessie's own. The editorialist's expression was perfectly deadpan.

"What about the men who attacked your shop?" asked Ki, who stood next to them with arms folded across his muscular chest. Coulter shrugged. "Local workingmen expressing their just outrage at the scandalous opinions expressed in *The Freeman*," he said. "If anything, I count myself fortunate he hasn't taken action against *me*. He considers me a troublemaker."

Jessie shook her head. "A scandalous way to run a railroad," she said.

"But not," Coulter said with a smile, "particularly unusual. Don't you agree?"

"Unfortunately," Jessie said. She shook her head. "Well, we knew all along we couldn't count on Coates for anything like help. We'll just have to make our own destinies."

"We always do," Coulter murmured. "Not everyone realizes it, though."

He looked at her. "Whatever happens, I'm with you, for whatever benefit my good will and actions can provide."

"Thank you, Davey," she said, feeling warmth spread to her cheeks. Part of her wondered just what good a man who would not even defend his own livelihood might be able to do her and her embattled people. But she was genuinely pleased by his offer in spite of herself.

She hugged herself. It was unusually cool tonight. Perhaps a storm was moving in. "Let's go down," she said, "and see if business has picked up."

Whether they had decided to become sympathetic to the Temperance Army's aims, or simply felt intimidated by its presence, the Liberty's regular customers stayed away in droves the night of Sister Angela's appearance. Only a few dedicated rummies wandered in across the course of the evening, to soak up the cheapest stuff pouring and stare blearily at the dancing girls. Cordwainer played with twice his usual mad energy, trying to perk the place up. Instead it gave Jessie the willies; it was just too much like whistling past the graveyard.

David Coulter stayed an hour after they came down off the roof, then made his way back home. Jessie defiantly kept the saloon open until its customary closing time of two A.M., even though the last sot staggered out at 11:30 and no one else came in.

When the clock struck two Jessie stood up from the barstool she was perched on. "That's it," she said to Ki, who stood impassively in his usual post by the wall, "finally."

70

She wiped her forehead with her apron. Despite the evening's coolness, she was covered in sweat. *This waiting is getting to me,* she thought. *Waiting for . . . what?*

The redheaded dancer—Charity Anne, who had the calf eyes for Ki—emerged from the back with a wrap around her bare shoulders. She smiled at Ki, who stepped forward to meet her.

"Walk me home, Ki?" she asked.

He shook his head. "I must stay with Miss Starbuck."

"But Ki! All those strange people, throwing bricks through the window and such—it's more dangerous than ever."

"And that is why I must stay," he said. "I'm sorry."

Jessie waved a hand at them. "Go ahead, Ki," she said. "They haven't been able to work up the guts for anything beyond a little glass-breaking—and they know I've got that scattergun. I'll be fine."

As the last words left her mouth two shots cracked in through the planking they had nailed over the broken window that afternoon.

★

Chapter 9

"Terrible what happened," Chief Coates said, mopping his brow with his handkerchief. "Terrible. It's guns that do it, of course. That's why we don't permit people to carry them in our fair city."

Jessie turned from the window to look the white-haired police chief haughtily in the eye. She had dressed up in her "respectable lady" clothes today—and had her thoroughly illicit dagger tucked away in its garter holster by her thigh.

"*Somebody* was evidently carrying them, Chief Coates," she said. "Somebody no doubt connected with that gang of hooligans encamped across the river."

He shook his head. "Now, don't go jumping to conclusions, Miss Starbuck," he said. "The facts don't warrant any such conclusion. None at all."

"And what conclusions *do* they warrant, pray tell?" she asked in tones of poisonous sweetness.

He dabbed his forehead again. The morning's heat was heavy-handed enough to raise a sweat on the bronze statue of General Grant in the town square, and the police chief was perspiring with unusual vigor. Perhaps the high collar of his blue tunic was too tight.

"Shots fired into your premises by parties unknown under cover of night," he said. "No more, no less. Regrettable, Miss Starbuck. Regrettable indeed. I shall have my men look into it."

She cocked a finely arched brow at him. "The way they're looking into the death of Bryce, my bartender?"

"Exactly."

She made as if to rise. "Speaking of guns, Miss Starbuck," the chief said, "rumors have reached my ears that you have displayed firearms on occasion in your . . . establishment."

"And if I have, isn't that my business?" she asked, pinning him with a withering glare.

He shrank back visibly. "Yes, yes, certainly. Ordnance does not forbid possession of firearms, as long as one is a resident and does not carry them on the street."

His little blue eyes got smaller and harder. "Of course, Miss Starbuck, in your case the question of residency might conceivably arise. . . ."

"I own property inside the city limits," she said, "and I pay taxes on it. And I've certainly been residing there since I arrived in Center City."

"Yes, yes. Of course. And I might add, you are a most commendable and welcome addition to our community."

Jessie smiled and nodded, thinking, *Welcome to whom?* She was beginning to wonder whether Center City's police chief was shifty or merely deranged.

She rose. "Well, Chief Coates, I won't take up any more of your time."

He waved an affable hand. "Think nothing of it, my dear. My door is always open to you."

As she started out that open door he said, "Ahem—your people won't cause any . . . any trouble, will they? That Mexican fellow for example . . ."

Again, she refrained from correcting him. It would be fairly hopeless, she was sure, to try to make Coates aware of the distinction between Japanese and Chinese. And Chinese

73

enjoyed lower status than Mexicans. Better for Ki if things were left the way they were.

"We won't start trouble, Chief Coates," she said. Then she smiled. "But if trouble starts, we *will* finish it.

"Good day."

Jessie leaned her weight on the rag she had been using to polish the hardwood bar and shook her head. "That police chief of yours is surely a piece of work," she said. "I reported the shots fired into the Liberty last night, and what he wanted to know is if *we* were packing guns."

She had changed, gratefully and hurriedly, out of the hot encumbering wool of her formal garments. Despite the fact that she was doing scutwork, Jessie was packing, quite openly: her heavy-framed .38 rode in its holster on her right hip. The Temperance Army was nowhere in evidence outside at the moment. But from now on she wasn't taking any chances.

Perched on a stool, David Coulter shook his shaggy blond head. "At least he didn't try to stop me from wearing this in here," Jessie said, slapping the worn hardwood grips of her six-shooter. "Though I'd like to see him try and stop me, at this point."

"They tried to put through an ordnance forbidding ownership of guns within the city limits, period," Coulter said. "The townsfolk didn't go for that. Laws like that are an invitation to those entrusted with law enforcement to turn into an armed gang themselves, and run the town like a mob of despots. As has already happened so many times in the West."

"Why do people go along with that?" Jessie asked, shaking her head. "Agreeing to render themselves defenseless."

"Largely out of fear, I suppose," the publisher said with a shrug. "Gun restriction laws are the original and most pernicious of Jim Crow laws. After all, politicians played on people's fears of the large numbers of newly freed slaves moving out of the South to get them enacted. Here in Center City our own self-proclaimed community leaders tried to raise the specter of armed depredation by our own Negro

74

population, though in truth they're for the most part quiet and industrious."

"What do the politicians offer in exchange for the people's disarming themselves?"

"The protection of the police force," Coulter said, flat deadpan.

Jessie blinked at him. Then she put back her head so that her unbound hair fell down her back like a cascade of gold, and laughed. It wasn't a titter, nor a girlish giggle. It was a full-blown belly-shaking guffaw, filled with delight at the wide world's absurdity. A laugh such as her father might have laughed.

"Forgive me," she said, when the storm had passed. She dabbed at a corner of her eye with the hem of her apron. "It isn't really funny, I suppose. But the thought of Chief Coates protecting *anyone* is—"

She broke off, shaking her head, while fresh tears started at the corners of her eyes. Then she collected herself, and looked David Coulter square in the eye.

"Thank you, Davey," she said sincerely. "That's the first good laugh I've had since I came to this blinder-wearing, stiff-necked, self-righteous burg!"

His grin turned him into a schoolboy. "Glad to be of service, Miss Starbuck."

That night's custom was even sparser than before. The reason wasn't hard to ascertain: a crowd filled both Central and Sullivan outside the corner establishment. This was no distaff chorus of off-key temperance serenaders. This was an exclusively male mob, mostly young and rough-looking, listening to a succession of bull-voiced speakers booming temperance from a precarious perch atop an upturned nail barrel.

They were still going strong by torchlight when Jessie finally decided to give up and close the Liberty, an hour or so before the customary time.

"If the spirit of Christian charity beats in the hearts of these fine young men," commented Martin Cordwainer, standing on tiptoe to peep through cracks between the planks nailed over the front window, "the torchlight fails to discover it on their faces."

"Maybe that's just as well," Ki commented. From outside, the waves of oration beat against the planks like surf. The big solid front doors had been shut over the swinging saloon gate. "Your history tells us that when the Christian spirit truly moves your people, they show it by setting accused unbelievers on fire."

One of the dancing girls—Wanda, blond and assuredly not born that way, by the darkness of the roots of her pulled-back hair—covered her ears. "Mr. Ki, don't talk that way! That's blasphemy."

"Is it my speech which is blasphemous," he asked imperturbably, "or the actions it describes?"

Cordwainer grinned and applauded. "Touché!" he cried, and tottered for his balance. "A hit, a palpable hit!"

"What about Japanese history?" Jessie asked. "I don't recall that your people treated your Christians with much kindness."

"Kindness does not form much of the political makeup of my mother's people," Ki said without emotion. "And, of course, our early Christian converts were still Japanese, and they acted accordingly: they sought to seize power themselves."

"Maybe people are the same wherever you go," said Jessie.

"Though most people belonging to either of my heritages would deny that," Ki said, "it is probably correct."

"I note that the conspicuously attractive person of our crusade leader has yet to put in an appearance tonight," the piano player said.

"Neither has Center City's fine police force," Jessie said.

Everyone laughed at that. "What are we going to *do?*" asked black-haired Sally.

Something hard thudded against the planking that covered the window—a rock or brick half, likely. The people gathered by the front of the darkened saloon jumped and

76

shied away like frightened horses. All except for Jessie and Ki, who stood as if nothing untoward had happened.

"Fort ourselves up here for the night, I reckon," Jessie said. Some of the saloon's employees, like Cordwainer, lived in the establishment itself. Most of the dancers lived at the hotel down the street; other employees, like Andy the handyman and Charity Anne, had dwellings elsewhere. "Everyone is welcome to stay here."

Sally looked at Wanda, and then at Jessie. "Unroll the spare horse blankets," she declared. "*I'm* not going out there."

The staff turned away from the window to prepare to bed down. Ki held Jessie by the window with a look from his black eyes.

"Is this really what you intend?" he asked. "To wait here, passive, until the mongrels outside work themselves up enough to come dig us out?"

"You think that's likely?"

"What else do you make of Sister Angela's absence from the scene? She appears to have the habit of being elsewhere when her followers commit acts of violence."

"What are you proposing?"

"Go on the attack."

She laughed, low, shook her head. "How did I know that's what you were going to suggest?"

"Perhaps my teaching has begun to wear off on you."

"Your constant harping, more likely." She looked him in the eye. "What do you suggest we attack *with* Ki? Are we going to arm the dancing girls with broom handles and send them out in a headlong charge? Maybe Cordwainer can cover them with the Gatling gun I cleverly managed to hide in the attic. You and I can wave banners from the roof and cheer."

"A Gatling gun." Ki looked thoughtful. Normally he disdained firearms, but for all his warrior's code of courage he was no fool, and had a keen eye for the odds, as well as for evening them.

Jessie had learned enough of his background to guess that

that was because he was actually of *ninja* stock, from Japan's no-caste caste of pariah assassins. Though the *ninja* enjoyed about the same status as barnyard animals in Japan, secrecy was their stock in trade; the higher members of their clans often lived as *buke,* the warrior nobles of the Eight Islands, and were accepted as such. If he was just a samurai, ruses and unchivalrous weapons—Gatling guns, for instance—would be beneath his contempt. Ki had been born into a double life even without taking his half-American half-Japanese ancestry into account. Though samurai and *ninja* were polar opposites, he was both—and Jessie always figured if she could someday understand *that,* she'd begin to get a handle on Ki's enigmatic homeland.

Besides, she had a sneaking suspicion that his usual avoidance of firearms sprang from the fact that, when he had to kill someone, he liked to feel their blood on his knuckles.

"Surely you could purchase a Gatling gun," he said now, "and have it shipped here secretly."

"You think we're going to hold out here for weeks and weeks, like the Paris communards?" She shook her head. "And besides, these are citizens, taxpayers. We can't just mow them down in windrows on a city street without somebody asking questions."

He shook his head. "Your people are abrupt and harsh in many ways," he said. "It mystifies me, the way you shroud yourselves in legalisms."

"We're half your people, too, Ki."

He laughed quietly. "Sometimes that half seems more alien than others."

Charity Anne House stood well back from the others, shawl wrapped around her shoulders, watching.

She thought of Ki as her man. That was foolish; she understood from the first time she saw him that it would be trying to rope the wind to think of tying him down. But he was like no man she had ever known or even imagined, strong when he needed to be and gentle when she wanted him to be. He was no swaggering bully who slapped her down when she looked at him with two eyes at once, yet he was certainly no milk-fed weakling who wanted her to be his mother and tuck him behind her apron strings.

And he cared for her, he truly did. Yet seeing him talking there to the woman who was his employer, and so much more, Charity Anne knew without doubt which way his loyalties would swing if there was ever a conflict. Or rather, that for him there could never *be* a conflict.

Trying not to be bitter, she shook her head. "I'm not staying here," she muttered to herself. "But I'm not too eager to travel alone, either."

"I will help you," a soft voice lisped from behind her.

She jumped, turned. It was young Andy, big and round and soft, looking at her with fawn eyes.

For a moment her heart quailed. She did not dislike or despise Negroes. She just had trouble thinking of them as really being *people*. They were so unfamiliar; there had been few to be seen in the part of Pittsburgh where she was raised. They were different than she was, and that made her wary.

Yet she had known Andy for months now, knew him to be gentle and sincere in his childish way. She had heard stories of the unbridled lusts of Negro men, and mental defectives for that matter. But it was impossible to think of Andy as anything but a big gentle child.

"I will walk you home, Miss House," Andy said. "I am scared to be out at night by myself, too."

What good can he do? she wondered. *He's as scared as I am.* But she would feel better for the company. And who knew? Maybe his size alone would deter attackers.

"Let's go," she said quietly. "Out the back—and hope the crowd doesn't see."

To Charity Anne's surprise the mob didn't have the rear of the Liberty covered. Nor was anybody watching the alley.

With Andy bumbling after her like a heavy-footed ghost, clutching his rag bunny to his breast, Charity Anne slipped down the alley, away from Central. She could hear the shouts and chanting of the crowd at her back. Her heart fluttered in her throat like a captive bird.

At alley's end she stopped. Motioning for Andy to wait, she peered cautiously up and down the lightless street. The waning moon, still half-full above, hung out of sight below the roofline. Nothing moved between the black blanknesses of the buildings' false fronts.

She led off, around the corner, down the street, across a cross street, and down another alley. Distance and the two- and three-story structures of downtown Center City muffled the mob's noise. Andy whuffled like a winded horse, but didn't complain.

The walls of the alley pressed in like cliffs to either side of them. Charity Anne moved cautiously in the dark, picking her way, trying not to step in something unmentionable, or put her foot in a hole and twist her ankle. She was not as far out of her element as she might have been. She had sometimes run well after dark in the alleys of her native Pittsburgh. Her parents hadn't minded, mostly; oftentimes they seemed all but unaware of her existence.

For her, those times were better. It was when they remembered her that trouble started.

Easing around a stack of splintery crates waiting to be torn apart and salvaged—even the poorest wood was at a premium here in the nearly treeless heart of Kansas— Charity Anne released a gusty breath and dared believe that they had gotten away clean.

Then figures loomed up at the end of the alley, barely ten feet away. "Well, looky here," a nasal voice sneered. "It's one of them soiled doves from that there den of iniquity."

"Goddam whores," another voice said.

Behind her, Andy gave a high-pitched squeal and ran away at a stumbling gait, bouncing off the sides of the alley.

A figure stepped forward. A spill of gibbous moonlight along the street caught it, illuminating an incongruous well-tailored three-piece suit, a bowler hat, and a slab of jaw that seemed out of place set atop such a slight frame.

"Let the Negro go," the newcomer said.

The first voice guffawed. "Hell! I mean, tarnation, Mr. Brokaw, it's white meat we got a taste for anyhoo."

"Then take her," Dan Brokaw said. "She'll make a fine object lesson for those who seek to oppose the will of the Lord, as made manifest through our beloved Sister Angela."

"Amen," came a rough-throated chorus.

Hopelessly, Charity Anne turned and tried to run.

★

Chapter 10

The double doors of the saloon banged open. For a moment Ki stood in the doorway, silhouetted with his burden against the glaring morning sun outside. Then he stepped forward, into the Liberty, his slippered feet making soft scuffling sounds on the planks.

Jessie brushed blond hair back from her face and left the heel of the hand pressed against her forehead as Ki strode forward and deposited his limp burden on the bar. Matted dark red hair spilled out one end of the rolled blanket. As Ki set the bundle down, the blanket slipped open. A white arm, streaked with blood and dirt, flopped free to hang down beside the bar.

Bottle-blond Wanda had pressed forward to see. Now she reeled away with a choking cry, and vomited on the floor.

Martin Cordwainer had been roused early from his customary alcoholic stupor by the commotion in the saloon that ensued after Jessie heard kids yelling in the street that a woman's body had been discovered several blocks away. He stood near the bar, blinking owlishly.

"Poor child," he said, shaking his head. "She looks like a kitten run over by a stagecoach."

Sally stood her ground, looking down at her friend. "What happened?" she demanded.

"She was raped," Ki said, stone-faced and oblivious to the gasps his use of an unspeakable word elicited from the female members of the company—except Jessie, of course, who was made of sterner stuff than most Victorian women. Men, too, if it came to that. "Repeatedly, by appearances. And beaten to death."

"Andy!" gasped brunette Arabella, who was dabbing Wanda's mouth with a rag.

Grimly, Ki shook his head. "The mob," he said.

"How can you be sure?" Sally asked.

He transferred his gaze to her. His eyes were like obsidian spearpoints. Jessie gave her points for not flinching away from them.

"You wish details?" he asked in a grating voice. Hastily she shook her head and backed away. Ki turned to Jessie.

She stepped up to stand in front of him with her back to the others. Very quietly she was shutting them out of the conversation. Catching the hint, Sally turned and went off for a bucket of water and a brush while Arabella escorted Wanda rubber-legged up the stairs to lie down.

"I claim the right of revenge," Ki said, pitching his voice so that only Jessie could hear.

She shook her head. "Ki—"

"She was one of ours," he said. "When was it the Starbuck way to leave their people unavenged? Is that not what binds us here in the first place?"

She held up her hands. "Ki, listen to me, *please*. She is—was—one of my people, and you know damned well I don't forget a thing like that. Getting justice for poor Bryce was one reason I chose to stick here in Center City. As was making sure none of my other employees was victimized."

She made a bitter mouth. "And I've done a poor job of that, it seems."

"Will you not let me act, then?"

"Act against *whom*, Ki? Do you know who did this? You can't even be sure it was Sister Angela's bunch—no, I know, I'm as sure of it as you. But we don't *know*."

"The one who calls herself Sister Angela leads that pack of dogs," Ki said. "She is accountable for their actions."

And in Japan that means she would pay with her head for something like this, Jessie realized. "We don't do things quite that way here, Ki."

He gestured with a callused hand toward Charity Anne's sad, partially covered corpse. "Perhaps that is why such things happen here."

She bit her lip. "Maybe. But think about this: Coates is watching us like a cat at a mousehole. I suspect that if anything happened to Sister Angela he wouldn't be quite as nonchalant as he was about Bryce or the midnight gunshots—or as I'm sure he's going to be about this. And it's you—since he's got you pegged as not being a white man—he's going to lay the hard arm on."

Ki shrugged. "I care not for myself."

"No. But what about me? If you get your silly posterior clapped in the *juzgao*, where does that leave *me*? Alone with that bunch out there, unless you think Martin and the dancing girls are going to be a lot of help when the chips are down."

She gestured toward Central, though by dawn the mob outside had melted away like fog. She had no illusion that it would stay dispersed.

He set his jaw. But then his shoulders sagged, and she felt the fight go out of him.

She put a hand on his chest. "Ki," she said, "Charity Anne will be avenged. So will Bryce. You know I'll never let this rest. Unless we *all* wind up needing to be avenged. But we have to handle this my way."

He drew in a deep breath, pressed it out explosively, as if delivering a blow. Then he nodded.

"Good," she said, reaching up to touch his dark cheek. "I knew I could count on you. I always can."

She looked around. Wanda's breakfast had been cleaned up. Martin Cordwainer was unsteadily pouring sawdust from a bucket on the wet spot on the floor. Jessie nodded. These were good people. Not extraordinary, not a collection of heroes and heroines. But steady.

Jessie knew she was extraordinary. She had been raised in the knowledge, and raised to take pleasure in the fact. To her way of thinking, and her father's before her, her special gifts imposed special responsibilities upon her. And that was as it should be.

Her father had also taught her never to look down on those who lacked her gifts. Because people like her could work enormous ill as well as good. If *everyone* was like her—or Ki, for that matter—she reckoned the world would be a far more turbulent place than it was already.

"Very well," she said. "It's time to arrange some disposition for poor Charity Anne. And then . . ." She sighed, and for a moment felt the pressure of tears at the backs of her eyes. She forced them firmly down.

"And then I'll march down to City Hall for my inevitably disappointing interview with the chief."

"Why, Fräulein?" Joachim Heinrich, Freiherr von Trott zu Pappenheim, stood behind Jessie where she sat alone at a table in the deserted afternoon saloon. Outside the Liberty the psalm singers had returned. An exclusively male chorus this time, and no faces Jessie recognized as being local. Which might have meant much or little; she didn't know all that many of Center City's residents on sight.

Jessie was again comfortable, in jeans and a man's shirt. She had a bandanna tied around her hair; there were chores to do. Pappenheim's long, pale fingers hovered above Jessie's shoulders like a pianist's hands above a keyboard.

"Why do you persist in staying here? Surely it is . . . *beneath* you, to put yourself in danger for a mere saloon."

He dropped his hands to her shoulders, began to knead her trapezium muscle with his powerful fingers. She moaned in

85

pleasure, let her head loll on her neck muscles.

"That feels good, Joachim," she said, almost purring. Then she sighed.

"You don't know how much I'd love to put this place behind me," she said. "But I can't, until this matter's settled."

"But what can be so important about the Liberty, to bind you here?" the young nobleman asked. "My foremost concern is for you. But what of the others—your employees, the townspeople—who will be put into danger if the storm now gathering outside of town should break?"

She patted his hand. "I know what you mean," she said, "don't think I don't, Joachim. I know I already got poor Charity Anne killed. I don't want more blood on my hands."

The interview with Chief Coates had gone about as she'd expected. Center City's top lawman had deplored the tragedy—and insisted that Jessie not leap to any conclusions about who was responsible.

"It might have been one of your own patrons, maddened by the Demon Rum," he had told her, mopping at the sweat beads gathered on his pink forehead.

"They must have had the longest enduring drunk in history, then," she replied coolly, "because I had scarcely a customer all day yesterday."

"Certainly, certainly," Coates said. "But that's merely a possibility. Didn't she leave your establishment in the company of that Negro fellow? And he hasn't been back to work today, I understand."

"It wasn't Andy," she said, fixing him with an ice cold gaze. "If you knew anything about him, you'd know he was incapable of any such deed. He's the gentlest person I've known in my whole life."

Chief Coates had only managed to meet her eyes for a split second before he looked nervously away. Jessie's denial that Andy might be responsible for the crime was based on pretty flimsy evidence. Nonetheless she was certain she was right—and if evaluating evidence was the

Chief's strong suit, he'd done a fine job of hiding it to date.

"Perhaps," he said, "perhaps indeed. I shall initiate an investigation."

"I cannot tell you how much that comforts me."

"I don't want more *innocent* blood on my hands," she continued. "But Charity Anne's murder makes me more determined than ever to stick it out here."

She tipped her head back to look up at him. An almost petulant look disfigured the classical perfection of the baron's features. Jessie laughed out loud.

He stepped back scowling. "Don't look so ferocious," Jessie scolded. "It makes you look like an angry child."

Pappenheim performed a stiff, tight bow. "I am sorry if my demeanor displeases the Fräulein," he said.

She turned in her chair. "Did your leg come off in my hand?" she asked.

"Bitte?"

"When I pulled it. I was *joking* with you, you know."

The anger passed from his face like a cloud from before the sun. "Ah," he said, once more his smiling, debonair self. He bowed again, with a self-mocking air, like a character from a comic opera. "I merely misunderstood mademoiselle's intent."

"I reckon so," Jessie said, nodding. She relaxed, and was surprised at how tense the baron's brief lapse from character had made her. *Don't be foolish,* she told herself. *It doesn't mean anything. We all have our little episodes.*

Nonetheless, a trace of tightness remained between her shoulderblades. She did not ask the baron to massage it away.

"Is it not a waste of time and your talents?" Pappenheim asked.

"You're back on the Liberty again, aren't you?"

"Of course. It concerns me. You are responsible for the affairs of a worldwide business empire. And you are likewise a young woman of breeding, of intelligence.

Running a saloon is so . . . *common*."

She laughed again. "I won't claim to be one of the common people," she said, "but my daddy taught me not to go giving myself airs, either. I can't claim any such gentle birth as yours, Baron. My daddy was a rough-hewn man in many ways, and while his people were downright proud, nobody'd ever mistake them for noblemen."

She shrugged. "I was born rich. But what I have, I worked for and earned. My daddy saw to that."

She rubbed at a smudge on her forehead, laughed, and gestured around the empty saloon. "You think this is the first floor I ever swept? Or even the first hardwood bar I ever polished? What I reckon you'd call menial labor isn't my favorite thing in the world, Joachim, but one thing my daddy taught me well: it doesn't kill you."

"Perhaps, perhaps," Pappenheim said. He grinned, and was all schoolboyish again, this time in a pleasing, infectious way. "And I have bent my back to a few tasks which might surprise you, in my time."

"I bet," Jessie said. "But I'm not sure anything about you could actually *surprise* me."

He shrugged. "In any event . . . do you truly believe what you do here is, how would you say? Worth the doing?"

"How do you mean?"

He spread his long, fine hands. "To fight so, to keep a saloon open. So that the denizens of the town have the freedom to come in and drink themselves into a stupor, then go home and thrash their wives and kick their broods of squalling brats around the house."

She frowned, took a deep breath. "I wouldn't say that description fits most of our customers, Baron. Some, sure. But if a man is minded to slap his wife and kids around, don't kid yourself the booze *makes* him do it. From what I've seen of the world, if he's that way, he'll find an excuse to go ahead and do as he pleases, come hell or high water. The alcohol is an excuse, but it isn't a cause."

Pappenheim waved the objection away with an airy flick of the wrist. "What about the effects of alcohol on such as your piano player, Herr Cordwainer."

"It's his life, Baron. We did away with slavery in this country, remember?" She grinned. "Besides, it seems I've known you to tip a glass or two over the course of our brief acquaintance."

"But that is different. People such as ourselves—nobility in fact, if perhaps not in terms of the niceties of birth—we know how to comport ourselves. We are in control; we can sample vice without becoming its slaves. The common ruck cannot."

"I think you sell most people short, Joachim." She shook her head, laughed. "I try to imagine what my daddy would do if a passel of busybodied blue-noses tried to tell him he couldn't take a drink when and where he pleased. Ki would sure get his wish for action *then*."

The young nobleman raised his brows. "Your man is eager to initiate violence?"

"He's hankering to pay some debts," she said. Her own expression hardened. "And don't get me wrong, Baron—so am I. We Starbucks pay our debts. And we don't run from fights. And maybe *that's* why I'm sticking it out here until the bitter end."

"You are assuredly an extraordinary young woman, Jessie," the baron said. "If you will not be convinced—"

"I won't be."

He shrugged. "Then I fear I must plead the pressure of other engagements." He kissed her proffered hand and strode toward the double doors.

Just before he reached them they swung open to allow David Coulter to amble in. He nodded to Pappenheim. "Baron. Good afternoon. A pleasure to see you, sir."

"Ah, yes, likewise," Pappenheim said. He seemed to hesitate, look back at Jessie. "With your permission, I was taking my leave."

"Certainly." They nodded to each other. The young baron left.

Coulter stood a moment looking after him. Outside the street had filled with shadow; the sun was almost down. The gathering dusk seemed to be congealing the air by degrees. Flies buzzed around, heat-torpid but plentiful.

"I believe we're fixing to see some of the storms that have so far had the grace to avoid us," Coulter remarked. He walked into the saloon. "Good afternoon, Jessie."

"David. I'm glad to see you." She gestured at a chair. "Have a seat."

The young publisher shook his shaggy head. "Sorry, I can't stay. I'm putting a new issue to bed. I have composed what I trust is a stirring editorial in support of what you are doing here: vindicating our right to choose."

She laughed. "Davey, while right now I can use all the friends I can get, I'm not exactly going to feel it's a moral victory if some of the psalm-singers outside take time off to bust up your shop again."

"At this stage, I'm afraid they are hardly to be diverted from their immediate goal," he said. "Which I fear seems to be your destruction. I am sorry about what happened to Miss House."

Jessie just shook her head.

"I know that I need not try to impress you with the gravity of your situation here," he said.

"No, you don't." She sighed and looked hard at him. "You're not going to try to talk me into packing it in, too, are you?"

He looked startled. "By no means. I came to tell you that what you are about is something that has needed doing for quite some time. Our Sister Angela has had things all her way for too long. It's past time for someone to take a stand."

He looked grim. "Unfortunately taking stands has its cost."

"As General Custer found out a few years ago."

"Let us hope your only point of similarity to him remains an impressive head of yellow hair," Coulter sad.

Jessie laughed. "Thanks for giving me something to smile about."

Davey grinned. "My pleasure. I do have to be going. But

90

one thing more: with your permission I shall return as I can to help you guard over your establishment."

And what good will that do? part of her wondered. Nonetheless, she found herself smiling with genuine pleasure at the offer.

"Thank you, Davey," she said. "I appreciate it."

He bobbed his head and left her alone with her thoughts, the ghosts, and the thickening dark.

★

Chapter 11

The proprietors of the Pleasant View Hotel prided themselves on their dining room. It was handsomely appointed, with gold wallpaper above waist-high, dark-stained oaken wainscoting, imported across the Great Plains at substantial expense, and green shades on mirror-polished brass lamps lit by gas from the new gasometer which was the pride of the growing railroad town.

Nonetheless it came off looking almost shabby by comparison to its current occupants. Some wore their wealth openly, in the form of thumbtip-sized diamond stickpins, lordly bellies, and big cigars; others went for the understatement of elegance. But wealth and power had left their unmistakable impressions upon all but one of the dozen men who had reserved the chamber for their exclusive use.

So exclusive, in fact, that the silent liveried servants who glided back and forth ensuring that none ever wanted for food or drink were all as imported as the wooden paneling, brought in by the wealthy occupants to wait on them. They were men who were well aware, as most wealthy and powerful men were not, that servants had eyes and ears. And more to the point, mouths.

The one exception to all that splendor, muted and not so, sat at the foot of the table trying not to feel self-conscious. Dan Brokaw sat ill at ease halfway down one side of the long table, aglitter with fine crystal and spotless linen, and tried not to feel dowdy. *These are powerful men,* he told himself, *but the skill of my pen gives me dominion over even such as they. And in intellect I am as wealthy as any of them. I'm just as good as they are.*

At the table's resplendent foot a pinched and colorless man in a high collar sat reading from a stack of printed pages. They were printed on excellent paper, with high rag content. The men of the cartel never stinted themselves.

"Our program," he said in a thin, rachitic voice, "continues to meet with success on all fronts." The pinched man's name was Billingsley. He was one of Boston's foremost financiers.

"The days of untrammeled competition are past," Billingsley continued. "The time has come for the state to take all of enterprise under its wing—under the wise and benevolent guidance of such men of firm will and probity as ourselves."

"Laissez-faire," said Toland, the rail magnate, laying down the Cornish hen he was devouring whole on his fine china plate and wiping grease from his several chins with an Irish linen napkin. "By which we now mean, 'let the state be up and doing!'" He belched enthusiastically.

Billingsley shot him an evil look. "It is our grand design, therefore—"

"Enough."

At the rasped word all heads turned to the man seated across the table from Brokaw. The other members of the cartel held tycoon Dennis Chester Luther Mellrooney to be an enigma. His fortune, it was understood, was primarily in livestock. However, he was rumored to have tentacles in almost all fields of endeavor, much like the cartel itself, that international brotherhood of the wealthy and powerful of which a portion had gathered tonight to discuss the progress of a vital pilot program. He was a small man, with a chalk-pale, immobile face and a body that seemed curiously lumpy beneath his black vest and coat.

"We use our puppets in the state and the press to make our rivals out as rapacious monsters, in order to cover our own rapaciousness," he said in his buzzing, curiously uninflected voice. "We all know that. Get to the meat of the matter."

Billingsley pinched his already almost nonexistent lips to a bloodless line. He was not used to being ordered about like a menial. Yet he said nothing.

"Snob has something on everybody here," murmured Mascomb, the manufacturing magnate who sat to Brokaw's left. It was he who had called this convocation. Despite the vast differences in their standing, he had taken the former reporter under his wing for the evening. Brokaw was there, in effect, as Mascomb's guest, and the tycoon seemed to enjoy having someone to show off his knowledge to. "Poor Billingsley hates like poison to be interrupted. But he daren't say a word."

"Our plan of covertly inciting union violence is beginning to bear fruit," Billingsley said crisply, flicking his eyes from Mellrooney to his pages reluctantly, as if expecting that if he only glared at his rival a little longer, the mysterious tycoon would burst into flame. "This is already having the desired effect of inciting employers—those who are too shortsighted to be invited to join our select number, or too obstinate—into using ever more harsh and desperate methods in dealing with the unions. This in turn convinces the working man that his bosses are arbitrary and vicious, and that a strong union is their only safeguard against an employer's whims."

He removed the top page, laid it precisely down, and allowed himself a juiceless smile. "Naturally, when the bulk of our nation's workers are unionized, it will be simplicity itself to control them. We merely co-opt or coerce selected union officials, and our will is done. At the same time we have one more weapon to use against those who oppose us."

"Brilliant, brilliant," murmured Lord Landsmere, the bejeweled Englishman who sat on Brokaw's other side.

"*I* don't think so," Toland said, mopping his brow with his napkin. "Damned anarchists are running wild everywhere. Even inciting my own workers. Ungrateful swine."

Mellrooney looked at him with dead black eyes. "Surely you know how to deal with such annoyances? Murder half the troublemakers. Frame the other half. Replace them with men you trust to stay bought."

"Voilà," said Rance Beauregard of New Orleans, who claimed distant kinship to the distinguished if failed Southern general, and liked to pretend to actually be French. "It's simple if you use your wits, Tully."

Toland glared at him. Some of the other magnates allowed themselves discreet smiles, Brokaw noticed. He gathered Toland was not the most respected of their number. That was his hole card, as it were, in this circle of powerful men: his journalist's eye. He was convinced journalists saw more clearly than other men. Even millionaires.

Particularly millionaires, perhaps. Brokaw was convinced they were mostly crass fools, unworthy to wipe the mud from the boots of a man of wisdom and discernation such as himself. It was the journalists who really knew what was what in the world.

Which made his dancing attendance on this assemblage of plutocrats all the more curious. Yet he was drawn to them. Clearly it was because they were undeniably a cut above the ruck of wealthy men—they saw with clear eyes and thought with clear heads, even the gross Toland, that cartoon capitalist with the pigeon egg-sized diamond stickpin and grease dripping down his chins.

They knew and understood power, *real* power. They understood it, and knew how to acquire more. And Brokaw knew in his secret heart that his skill with the pen gave him unacknowledged power, over even the likes of these men— even enigmatic Mellrooney.

By helping them, then, he was helping himself. When they held all power, *he* would have his share. And covertly, meaning that he would bear no blame for failures of policy or will, and not attract the potentially lethal intrigues of those who coveted his position, because he would *have* no position, not visibly. He could play the power behind the thrones. Such was the power of the press, in the brave new world he was helping to build.

He felt eyes upon him. Dry-stick Billingsley was gazing right at him as he gummed out words: " . . . press campaign is coming along well. The muckrakers we support with secret payments and encouragement do much to blacken the names of our rivals."

Brokaw caught himself starting to frown. These men were lumping *him* with common scandal-mongers. He made his wide mouth smile, made his high forehead bob acknowledgement. *Let them underestimate me,* he told himself. *It will make my way that much smoother.* Yet in his stomach the fine foods he had eaten commenced to roil like swamp muck.

"All very well, Billingsley," came Mellrooney's voice, cutting across the grain of the secretary's words like a mill-saw, "but how about getting to why we have gathered here tonight in this inconvenient location."

"So far from the civilized amenities," added Toland, waving a leg he had just wrenched from the carcass of a new bird. Grease glistened on grey flesh around the cartilage knob at the leg's end.

"As usual your preoccupation with your gut overwhelms your wit, Tully," Beauregard said. "What's important is that we've all been dragged far from the seats of power."

Mellrooney looked at him. The flat blankness of chalky face and coal eyes was itself contempt, as if the mystery tycoon could not be bothered even to sneer. "Where the telegraph lines run, *there* is power," he said. "I wanted an accounting of why we were compelled to the inconvenience of traveling to this place."

"Mellrooney hates to leave New York," Mascomb said, pitching his voice low. But not so low, Brokaw realized with something like alarm, that the subject of the aside could not clearly hear it across the table. "Hates it like poison. They say he has himself quite the pleasure dome in his penthouse in Manhattan. Though not exactly what you'd call *stately*."

"A ridiculous rumor," Beauregard said across the table. "Our esteemed Snob has no weaknesses, it's well known. Certainly he has no eye for the ladies."

Brokaw, who had made it a point to amass all the knowledge he could of these powerful men, knew that the New Orleans magnate himself had a notable bent in that direction, and was supporting no fewer than three mistresses in apartments in the French Quarter. He remained somewhat alarmed to be party to such an intimate discussion of such a creature as Mellrooney; that the mysterious plutocrat's ruthlessness approached an Arab potentate's was perhaps the one concrete fact known of him. Yet Mellrooney had turned his strange face back to Billingsley, and was ignoring the conversation, as if it concerned the goings-on on the backside of the moon.

Brokaw felt a thrill then, in the pit of his kettle-like little paunch, around the base of his scrotum. Here was *real power*. It was intoxicating as some Oriental drug.

"Feller's not subject to le vice, either, insofar as anyone can ascertain," added Lord Landsmere. He used the British schoolboy pronunciation of the French, so that it came out to rhyme with *free ice*. Rance Beauregard rolled his eyes with theatrical disdain.

"It's all a sham," whispered Mascomb behind a knowing hand. "As soon as he's out of our sight, he'll make a beast of himself, mark my words."

Billingsley was glaring at them with intense dry heat. "If you have all finished with your schoolboy gossiping, perhaps I can provide Mr. Mellrooney—and such of the

97

rest of you as may be interested—with the answer to his question."

He turned his gimlet gaze on Brokaw. "Or rather, our agent on the scene, Mr. Brokaw can."

Resisting a sudden desire to loosen his high paper collar, Brokaw nodded and rose. "Gentlemen, the popular evangelist who calls herself Sister Angela is the focus of one of our most ambitious and far-reaching experiments," he said. He hesitated slightly, just at the first, but quickly found his footing. Here was his familiar ground, words; he knew how to make them work for him. They were *his* source of power. "I should mention at this juncture that Sister Angela is herself quite innocent of the manner in which she is being used, or indeed of the existence of such an august body as this. She is really quite childlike."

"At least in some ways," the Englishman said.

Brokaw swallowed but did not glance at the nobleman. "First," he went on, "the Temperance Army provides an invaluable pilot project in learning to control the masses, through religion, through the use of emotionally charged words, through manipulation of the mob phenomenon, and in the fair person of Sister Angela herself, shall we say, lower feelings."

"She has a lovely neck, indeed," murmured Lord Landsmere.

Brokaw felt his cheekbones beginning to burn at the Britisher's Victorian-veiled reference to the evangelist's impressive frontage. Sister Angela was a tool, a mere puppet in Brokaw's hands. But she was *his* puppet. It wasn't right for this wealthy overbred fop to say such things about her.

He forced his mind back on-track. The least of these men—which Lord Landsmere was far from being—could squash him like a bug. And not recall it tomorrow.

"S-second," Brokaw said, and cursed himself with silent savagery for stuttering, "it is a way of beginning to erode at the pernicious and outmoded concept of *rights*, which the founders of this country saddled it with. Just as every lout regards his home as his castle, he regards his schooner of beer or shot of rotgut as a privilege bestowed by God."

"I shall thank you to refrain from blasphemy, Mr. Brokaw!" Billingsley's voice rapped, like knuckles on a desktop.

Brokaw felt his cheeks flush again. He swallowed, nodded. "I'm sorry, Mr. Billingsley. I misspoke. Forgive it."

He was thinking, *And you're not immune to the blandishments of le vice, you shriveled old sodomite. I know all about your little collection of Episcopal choirboys.*

"In any event, we are hoping to use the temperance movement—exemplified by Sister Angela's Temperance Army—as a tool to bring about the prohibition of alcohol. If the public can be made to acquiesce in that, we shall be well on our way toward making them submit to other forms of control which they would now find unthinkable."

"And anything we don't *make* 'em do," Mascomb said with a sly grin, "we'll forbid 'em doing!"

"You have a fine grasp of the obvious, Mascomb," Mellrooney said.

Mascomb's eyes flashed. Then his plump cheeks quivered, ever so slightly, and he drew his head fractionally down into his collar. After a moment, Brokaw decided it was safe to continue.

"Finally, when the public's enormous thirst for alcoholic beverages cannot be legally quenched, an enormous market for contraband liquor will spring into being overnight." Mascomb had carefully coached him on this art, before the dinner began. He himself had nothing but contempt for such accountings of profit and loss. But they meant the world to *these* men. "Our estimates are such that the price of illicit alcohol will double or even quadruple. With the breweries and distilleries we have begun to purchase or build in Canada, and the smuggling channels we have already prepared, we shall be placed to reap enormous advantage."

"Hear, hear!" sang out Toland, gesturing with his wineglass.

Brokaw felt Mellrooney's eyes upon him. His own skin crawled, as if to the touch of insect feet.

"I am given to understand that an obstacle has recently appeared in our path," the magnate said.

"A most *familiar* obstacle," added Lord Landsmere. "One might even say, overly familiar."

Toland snorted laughter. "Don't you wish!"

Landsmere blushed. "Gentleman," snapped Billingsley. He glared them to silence, then looked back at the former newsman. "You may continue."

"Sister Angela's current target," Brokaw said, "lies in the town of Center City, not many miles from where we sit. It is a saloon called the Liberty."

"We dragged ourselves out here into the wilderness for this?" Toland demanded. "Over a saloon?"

"Hear him out, Tully," said Mascomb, who was visibly getting some of his sauce back. He glanced at Mellrooney as if for support. The tycoon nodded once.

"What is exceptional about the Liberty is who owns it," Brokaw said. "None other than that long-time thorn in our collective sides, Miss Jessie Starbuck, heiress to the Circle Star empire."

A cicada hissing circled the table. That was an all too familiar name indeed.

"Really, Mr. Brokaw," rasped Billingsley above the disapproving noise, "I wish you would not insist on speaking of yourself as if you were one of us. If you wish to find a secure place in the society we are about building, you would do well to remember your place."

Brokaw stared down at the tablecloth. It felt as if a flannel rag clogged his throat, and his cheeks burned. "Yes, sir," he muttered.

Of course, he reminded himself, *the path to such power has its sacrifices.* Such as appearing to fawn upon these men. The time would come when they would properly appreciate the power of the press. Like any useful tool it cut both ways. But for now he had to swallow his pride.

100

"Go on," Mellrooney urged. "Speak however you wish. I have no time for trivia."

Brokaw longed to glance at the stick-dry Philadelphia magnate to see how he liked being put in *his* place. He didn't dare. Instead he cleared his throat and continued.

"An advance party of the Temperance Army manhandled an employee of the Liberty," Brokaw said, "to the effect that the man expired. Miss Starbuck decided to take a personal interest in the matter, and came herself to Center City. She actually traveled to the place the Temperance Army was encamped to defy Sister Angela in person."

He smiled. "Sister Angela has decided to pick up the gauntlet. The Temperance Army has shifted to Center City, where it holds the Liberty in a virtual state of siege."

Toland had his head down. He wagged it side to side, making his jowls quiver like jelly. "I still don't understand," he said. "All this fuss over a saloon?"

"The point is not the *saloon*," Mellrooney hissed. "It is the opportunity it provides to deal once and for all with that persistent menace, the Starbuck woman."

"Yes, yes indeed," said Mascomb, smiling all over his face. "And thank you very much, Mr. Brokaw. You have done well."

The newspaperman blinked, taken aback by being so summarily dismissed. He sat back down.

"To further explain both this magnificent opportunity and the means by which we plan to avail ourselves of it," he said, nodding toward the figure which sat, unspeaking, with a half-smile of amusement, at the table's far end from Billingsley. Unlike the others in the room, the figure was youthfully slim, and seemed to vibrate with controlled energies.

"Without further ado, gentlemen," Mascomb said, "permit me to introduce one of the key architects of our plan for world domination—a man who despite his tender years is a personal political advisor to Prussia's Prince Bismarck himself: Joachim Heinrich Jürgen Maria, Freiherr von Trott zu Pappenheim."

★

Chapter 12

"Where you think you're goin', tar-baby?"

Andy stopped and clutched his rag bunny closer to his broad overall-clad chest. Guilt—over running off and abandoning Miss Charity Anne, over not coming in to work for two whole days—had driven him from hiding, back toward the Liberty. He had thought he would be safe enough, slipping through the alleys. He knew Center City's alleys well; he had used them most of his life, to avoid the crowds of children who seemed to delight in taunting him—even though he knew inside that he was really one of them.

The alleys had served him well again—until he was a scant block from Miss Jessie's saloon.

He looked behind him. White faces walled him in from behind as well, fisted and unfriendly. But the faces that showed anger did not scare him so much as the ones that smiled.

Tears began to stream down his cheeks. "No, no," he wailed, shrinking to the side. "Please don't hurt me! I din't do nothin'!"

The one who had called him "tar-baby" was young and moist-lipped, with a lock of yellow hair hanging in blue eyes. Malevolence glinted in them like sun on steel.

He pushed Andy in the chest. The young black man staggered back against a wooden wall.

"It's not what you *did,* nigger," the blond youth said, "it's what you saw."

"Din't see nothin'!"

"Oh, yes you did. You saw white Christian men, out doing the Lord's work. And it might just creep into that shriveled rabbit turd you call a brain to bear witness against us."

Andy shook his head, too terrified for words. The yellow-haired youth reached out and plucked the doll from his hands.

"No!" wailed Andy, grabbing for the toy. "Gimme that! She's mine!"

The blond youth danced back, laughing. "You love this piece of rag, huh? Well then, I guess we oughta tear it to pieces." He grabbed it by the head and tried to twist it off.

"Daisy Bunny!" Andy cried. He grabbed for the doll, caught the blond youth by the arm.

"Get your paws off me, you filthy nigger!" the boy shrieked. He punched Andy in the nose with his free hand. Andy staggered back, clutching his face, blood streaming between splayed fingers.

"Somebody burn this piece of trash," the blond boy said. He tossed the rag rabbit to the knot of Temperance Army faithful blocking the alley mouth.

A tall figure stepped in front of them. A pale hand deftly caught the thrown toy.

"You shouldn't trifle with other people's property, boys," said David Coulter calmly.

"Hey, it's that nancy-boy free-thinker editor!" exclaimed a local recruit, a loose skinny youth in his twenties.

"I'll teach you to stick your skinny nose where it don't belong, nigger-lover!" exclaimed a heavyset older man who had hit town with the army. He aimed a scarred fist at the target he'd named.

Midway there Coulter's hand reached out and caught the fist. "I have had," he said, "a sufficiency of you intolerant louts."

He twisted the captive fist. The burly man squalled, dropped to one knee. The editor kicked him smartly in the pit of his stomach. The temperance soldier rolled over, clutching himself and retching.

The skinny boy came up behind Coulter and grabbed his shoulder. Without looking, the publisher slammed his elbow up and back into the boy's face. There was a splintering sound. The boy sat down hard, holding a mouth that gushed blood like a fountain.

"You busted my teef!" he cried out. Broken white chunks drooled from the ruin of his mouth. He began to cry.

Coulter paused, took off his thick, square-framed glasses, folded them carefully, and tucked them in the breast pocket of his tan suit. Then he stalked toward the blond young man who had punched Andy. The rag bunny dangled casually from one fist. The local recruits to Sister Angela's cause— some of whom had participated in forays against *The Freeman*—for the first time took note that what they had always assumed were just a soft sissy-boy's hands were in fact anything but. They were large and powerful, with enlarged knuckles.

The blond youth stood balanced on the balls of his feet, rubbing up his own knuckles. "You just bought yourself a wagonload of hurt, Mister."

Coulter ignored him. "Here," he said to Andy as he approached. "Keep a good hold on her."

He tossed the rag doll to Andy. The large boy caught her and held her tight, bubbling over with tearful gratitude. Then his gaze slid past the tall man's shoulder and his eyes got wide.

In a single sinuous motion Coulter ducked, weaved, and stepped out of the way as a Temperance Army tough ran at him from behind, swinging a length of board at the back of his head. The board instead struck the blond youth smack in the middle of the forehead. It laid scalp open to white bone and dropped him like a cannonball.

Coulter straightened. "Looks as if you delivered that wagonload of hurt to the wrong address, young man," he said to the startled temperance soldier, who stood staring at his leader's bleeding head in adenoidal dismay. He plucked the board from the young man's hands.

The young man snapped out of his daze and cocked a fist. Taking the board with his own two hands about the width of his shoulders apart, he dropped it crosswise behind the temperance warrior's head. With a sudden heave he dragged the youth's face downward to meet his rapidly rising knee. Teeth and bone crunched and the young mob member collapsed in a welter of blood and splinters.

Coulter looked down at him and shook his head sadly. "I fear good manners are in decline," he said. Raising his head, he blinked mild blue eyes at the mob. "Does anybody else feel the need of moral instruction?"

The ringleader reared to his knee. His blond hair was matted and lank with blood. He touched his split scalp and howled.

"There's only one of him to a dozen of us, you ninnies," he shouted. "Pile on the son of a bitch!"

From Sullivan and Central came the monotonous droning of hymns. The Temperance Army was maintaining its siege of the Liberty round-the-clock now. Despite that fact, the customers had begun to filter back into the saloon, usually in pairs and threes. Conversation over drinks had a muted, defiant air.

Ki was carrying a crate of trash into the back alley when his warrior senses, honed keen as an ancient *katana* by years of training and practice, caught the sounds of a scuffle from the next block.

He frowned, and set the crate down on top of a stack of similar ones. When the situation cleared up, they would rent a wagon and haul the debris to the town dump. The wood in the crates was far too valuable to be allowed to go to waste.

He wiped sweat from his forehead. The day was hot and muggy in that special way which portends a cloudburst on the Plains, and the clouds were beginning to pile up to the east, threatening gunmetal masses, the high-altitude winds commencing to plane their tops into the distinctive anvil shapes of thunderheads. A storm was due to break soon over Center City—and that didn't just mean weather.

The commotion might be a sign of the gathering storm. Ki's impulse was to go and investigate, on the basis that anybody who might run afoul of Temperance Army gangs would be a likely ally. But Jessie was inside the Liberty, and so was his duty.

Then he heard a high-pitched wailing, which he recognized as the voice of Andy.

That changed things. Jessie was inside, but she was armed, not alone, not immediately under attack, and fairly well able to take care of herself. Ki's secondary responsibility, after keeping Jessie safe, was the safety of Circle Star employees. It might have been a thin rationalization, but it was all he needed to get him started sprinting down the alley and up the block.

An alley away a gang confronted Andy, who was huddled against the wall clutching his rag bunny and weeping helplessly. Between him and the circle of angry white faces was the lanky figure of David Coulter, the pacifistic free-thinker and editor.

Except he was acting like no pacifist Ki had ever met. He was wading through the gang of temperance toughs dealing blows with a deadly precision that didn't fall far short of Ki's own.

Coulter held his hands right before the center of his body, half extended, and moved them with remarkably economy. Ki watched him block two punches to his face with slight turnings of his bony wrists. Then the publisher's fists drummed a quick tattoo on his attacker's face, three sidewinder strikes of either fist, that sent the man reeling backwards to collapse in a pile of debris.

Another man caught him roughly around the neck from behind. Without looking he slammed a backfist over his shoulder into the man's face. As the man fell back holding his nose, Coulter met a blow at his stomach with an across-the-body palm heel block that struck with a sound like a gunshot. That man squealed like a horse in a burning barn, and staggered back, clutching a forearm from which the hand dangled loose.

Despite being badly outnumbered, the apparently inoffensive publisher was quickly gaining the advantage. The temperance goons were getting the same idea. Ki saw a small, black-bearded man lurking at the rear of the group reach inside his coat and bring out a short-barreled revolver with a blue finish.

So far Ki had seen no reason to interfere. It would hardly be respectful for Ki to get involved, since that would imply Coulter needed help, which he clearly didn't. Or hadn't—the gun changed things.

Ki's hand snapped down. A many-pointed metal star dropped into his hand. He whipped his arm up and then forward as the bearded man leveled his pistol, trying for a bead on the unsuspecting Coulter.

The *shuriken* buried itself in the back of the man's gun-hand. The bearded man yelped, dropped the gun, and stood staring at his hand in horrified disbelief.

Ki began walking purposefully forward. The black-bearded man yelped again and ran straightaway up the alley away from him. The rest of the group followed until only the ringleader with the split-open scalp remained. He bared his teeth in an animal grimace and went lurching off after his followers.

"Evidently they felt the two of us outnumbered them," Coulter said, smiling at Ki. He took his glasses from his pocket, carefully unfolded them, and placed them back on the bridge of his nose. "My thanks for dealing with the boy with the gun, Mr. Ki."

Ki nodded briskly.

Coulter stooped, picked up the abandoned revolver. "Merwin & Hulbert, .32 caliber," he said. "Not a very popular piece. Capable enough of doing damage though. We'll not leave this lying about."

He straightened, slipping the blue revolver into a pocket. Then he patted Andy on the arm. "Here, lad. Let's see you safely to the Liberty. Or do you wish to go home?"

Andy sniffled. "I wanna go home."

"Then we shall escort you," David Coulter said.

Ki frowned. "I should not leave Miss Starbuck alone for so long."

"I—I be okay alone," Andy said. "I run straight home."

Coulter looked from the youngster to Ki and frowned. "If you're sure, Andy."

"You could go with him," Ki said.

Coulter shook his head. "There might be legal repercussions arising from our little encounter. How will your word, alone, stand up against the testimony of a half-dozen God-fearing white men prepared to lay hand upon the Bible and lie like congressmen? I'm not the best-respected man in town, but of all the things I've been accused of, not being a white man in good standing is not one of them. Deplorable that matters should be conducted on such a basis, but there you have it: I stand a fighting chance of being believed. You won't be."

Ki didn't have an answer to that one. "Andy knows his way around town quite well," Coulter went on. "I suspect it was only because the mob was patrolling the area around the Liberty that he ran afoul of them."

He turned to the youngster. "You're sure you can get home safely?" The young man nodded, eyes huge. "Then go. And be sure you tell your folks everything that happened."

Andy turned and headed off at a lumbering run, Daisy Bunny dangling from the crook of his arm. Coulter watched him go, thin-lipped. "Poor lad. I hope I'm not making a mistake by not going with him."

They headed back toward the Liberty. Ki kept alert without being obvious about it, and it took his warrior's perceptions little time to discover Coulter was doing the same thing.

"The way you fought, back there," Ki said. "I know Chinese boxing when I see it. I am unfamiliar with the style, but I thought to see echoes of Shaolin."

"Indeed," Coulter said. "It's a style called *wing chun,* comparatively little-known even in China. Are you familiar with the tale of the Venerable Five?"

"The five monks who escaped the destruction of the first Shaolin Temple by the Ch'ing, and perpetuated the knowledge of Shaolin fighting?"

Coulter nodded. "The very ones. One of them, though, was a nun, Ng Mui. She taught an abbreviated form of Shaolin boxing to a young woman named Yim Wing Chun. The girl, Wing Chun, elaborated the system, and passed it on under her name. It's not as flowery or elaborate as some Chinese forms, but it's quite efficient."

"So I can see." Ki looked sideways at Coulter. "Yet I thought the Chinese were reluctant to teach such secrets to . . . foreigners."

"*Gweilu,*" Coulter said with a smile. "White devils. What you would call *gaijin,* 'outside folk,' I think."

"You know much of Asia."

"I was raised there." They were walking down Sullivan toward the Liberty. The psalm-singers clumped down by the saloon paid them no mind.

"I was the son of a Yankee clipper captain on the China run. After my mother died, my father Jethro Coulter took me with him to sea. I was all of eight years old.

"With little left to call him home, my father decided to stay in Asia, building trade contacts. While he was off on a junket to Sarawak, I went sailing in a small boat with one of his father's employees. A junk full of South China Sea pirates chased us. Trying to escape them, we were caught up in a storm and wrecked on the coast. Chou was killed. I was rescued by villagers."

They reached the alley that ran behind the Liberty, turned down it after a brief scrutiny of the Temperance stalwarts.

They were all women, and showed no sign of interest in the two men. Probably they did not know either on sight, and would only have swooped down on them had they shown signs of wanting to enter the watering hole.

"An old woman took me into her care. She turned out to be a teacher of *wing chun*. For some reason she took a liking to the terrified little *gweilu* boy, and undertook to train him, so that he need never be frightened again."

At the back door they paused for Coulter to finish the tale. "After months of searching, my father located me. Raising a son was, frankly, proving a distraction to him; since the old woman and I had obviously formed a bond, my father arranged that she should continue to care for me and teach me."

He shrugged. "So I was raised, half-Chinese for all intents and purposes, training rigorously in *wing chun* and visited periodically by my father. I didn't come back to the States until I was seventeen, when Father was ambushed and killed by Sea Dyak tribesmen in Borneo."

Ki nodded. "Your teacher would be proud of you. You do her teaching honor."

David grinned. "I try. Now we'd best go inside and fill your fair employer in on what's gone on."

Jessie had just heard the tale of Andy's rescue when a pair of city police, wearing uniforms with double rows of mirror-polished brass buttons down the fronts, appeared in the swinging double doors.

"Miss Starbuck," said the shorter, stouter one, who sported an impressive set of russet-colored Burnsides, "we have a warrant for the arrest of your Mexican."

★

Chapter 13

"On what charges?"

He glanced at his partner, who was taller, thinner, paler, and younger. The other man stood fingering his nightstick, eyeing Ki with a curious combination of anticipation and dread. Apparently word of the half-Japanese's prowess was getting around.

"Assaulting peaceable white men," the stout one said. "Will you surrender him to us nice and peaceable-like."

"No."

The two exchanged glances again. The taller one got a shade paler and moistened his lips with a pink tongue.

"Resisting arrest is a serious charge, Miss," the stubby one said.

"Don't be absurd. Nobody is resisting anything."

"Does that mean you'll let him come with us, ma'am?" asked the younger cop.

"Certainly not. It means I am coming with you to Chief Coates at once, in order to clear this nonsense up."

• • •

"Herr Ki."

With the saloon to himself for the moment—and under strict orders not to set foot outside until his employer had set the Center City police department straight—Ki had moved the tables and chairs to the side of the room and was practicing *kata* on the bare plank floor. He paused with his hands crossed before his chest in the preliminary to a turning downward block.

The tall, slender Baron von Pappenheim stood in the doorway. His classically handsome young face was grave.

"I regret to inform you," the Prussian said, "that a terrible accident has befallen Miss Starbuck. You must come at once; she is asking for you."

Ki stood a moment, staring at him. He lived, for the most part, according to the classic samurai code of honor. It was a simple code, on the face of it: adherence to duty was absolute.

The real world, unfortunately, is anything but that simple and clear-cut. Ki found himself caught in the classic Japanese dilemma. Not duty versus human feelings, but *giri* versus *ninjo*; in such cases *ninjo* was supposed to loose, and that was that. Rather, he was caught in a conflict of duty versus duty. Feelings didn't enter into it—or so he assured himself.

He had been ordered to stay at the Liberty. He had a duty to obey Jessie. But now she needed him—and to his mind, his one overriding duty was to keep her safe, and orders be damned.

If he made the wrong choice, after all, he could kneel down and cut his guts out in the ritual of *seppuku*. No one ever said being samurai would be easy.

He nodded. "I will come."

"Chief Coates," Jessie said in a voice that purred menace, "this is the most outrageous thing I've ever heard."

Starting up from his desk, mopping his crimson face with a handkerchief, the chief said, "I couldn't agree more, Miss Starbuck—"

112

Jessie froze his words in his throat with an icy glare. She had taken time to put on her "respectable lady" outfit before marching down to the Town Hall. David Coulter stood behind her in the doorway of the chief's office.

"Hooligans are running wild in your town, raping and killing," Jessie said. "You have yet to lift a finger to do anything about it."

"But, Miss Starbuck, I am trying to do something about it. That's why I sent my men after that Mexican of yours. I have a report that he stabbed a man. That's the very sort of lawlessness I'm trying to put a stop to."

"He injured the hand of a man who was trying to pull a gun on me," Coulter said quietly.

Coates's eyebrows crawled up his forehead. "Why would he be pulling a gun on you, Mister, ahh, Mr. Coulter?"

"Because I interfered when a gang of Temperance Army ruffians was trying to beat one of our citizens to death, Chief." He smiled thinly. "I'm sure you'll agree I couldn't permit such a thing to happen."

Looking from Coulter to Jessie, Coates lowered his bulk back into his chair. "Which citizen would that be?" he asked almost plaintively.

"A Mr. Andy Jefferson. He's an employee of Miss Starbuck's."

"Oh," the Chief said. Then he brightened. "As matters would have it I've been looking for him, in connection with the murder of Miss House."

"Chief Coates," Jessie said sweetly, "do you actually understand who I am?"

He blinked, frowned. "Why, you're Miss Jessie Starbuck—"

"And a very rich woman, Chief."

"I'm, uh, I'm afraid I cannot allow that to influence me. Justice is blind, as they say."

"Our cowhands around the Circle Star have a word they use to describe statements like that," Jessie said. "My father always whupped me when I used it, however."

She walked around the desk to stand looking out the window at the town square. "Do not misunderstand me,

Chief. I am not attempting to bribe you. And far be it from me ever to try to divert Justice from her course."

She swung toward the Chief and crossed her arms. "In fact, I am so determined to see justice served that I am tempted to call upon certain influential friends of mine and my dear departed daddy's to get to the bottom of things."

She leaned close. "Which means, Chief, if I crook my little finger, a horde of lawyers, state legislators, and federal marshals will descend upon this town like a biblical plague of locust. But then . . ."

She straightened and half-turned away. " . . . I'm sure a man as upstanding as yourself would welcome such scrutiny."

The chief was perspiring even more freely than before. "Of course," he said.

He moistened his lips and looked at Coulter. "Well, sir, if you're willing to swear an affidavit to the effect that Miss Starbuck's man was only coming to your aid, I will rescind the order for his arrest."

Walking home from Coates's office, Jessie slipped her arm through Coulter's. "Thanks," she said.

He gave a little shrug. "I'd find it hard to live with myself if I just stood by and watched injustice done."

"It was good of you to take the blame for fighting with those men, though."

He grinned. "That was nothing but telling the truth."

She stopped, stared up at him. Down Central, the street in front of the Liberty was clogged with psalm-singers. Some of them were beginning to cast dubious glances at the pair approaching from the square, but they were showing no definite signs of hostility. *They don't recognize me in my "proper lady" duds,* Jessie thought.

"Surely you're kidding," she told Coulter.

He showed her a lopsided grin and shrugged. He didn't say anything.

It was his refusal to try to convince her that made Jessie wonder if he might in fact be telling the truth. Certainly, she hadn't noticed any tendency to lie in the handsome

114

blond-haired publisher. She untwined her right arm from his left, caught his hand, and studied it.

"Why, your knuckles are skinned!"

His grin turned rueful, and he shook his head. "I don't keep my hands tempered as well as I ought. Even if I still know better than to clout louts in the jaw with a closed fist, I managed to do myself some small hurt."

They began to walk again. Jessie had a vision of him wading into the midst of the mob assailing Andy, striking out wildly and inexpertly, like an angered stork. The picture wouldn't fit in her mind, somehow. All at once she couldn't square it with the quiet and casual confidence with which Coulter spoke of the fight. In fact, his manner reminded her of no one so much as Ki . . . or Longarm. *What's going on here?* she asked herself.

"There she is!" a female voice screeched. "The very whore of Babylon!"

"It seems your avid public has finally recognized you," Coulter murmured. He took Jessie's arm firmly.

"The woman in scarlet!" another woman cawed.

"Debaucher of innocence!"

"Here, now," Coulter said to the women. "Do you really want to let your zeal overwhelm your manners? Besides, your name-calling implies that I, as Miss Starbuck's current escort, am none other than the Beast of Revelations. Malefactor I may be, but surely more modest than all that."

Feeling her cheeks burn hot, Jessie faced the crinoline crowd that now blocked the way to her saloon. She felt an overwhelming urge to slap every one of those faces, pinched, sanctimonious, and hating beneath frilly bonnets.

"How can you stand there with your psalm books in hand," she said sharply, "when your menfolk are camped out by the river, working themselves up for another night of rape and murder?"

"Lies!"

"She defames what's good and true!"

"That is the Devil speaking through your lips, sister,"

said a tall woman with a face like an axe blade.

Grimly Jessie started for her. Coulter refused to relinquish her arm.

"Before I let you go," he murmured in her ear, "while I don't doubt you can lick the lot of them, are you sure you want to undertake to?"

Despite her fury, she laughed and shook her head. "You're right," she said. "It isn't worth it." She cocked her head and looked at him as if seeing him for the first time. "And if Old Nick's speaking through one of us, I reckon it must be you, with that silver tongue of yours."

"Between you and this crowd of admirers, my head's soon going to be turned," he said. "Shall we go inside?"

Jessie nodded her head, making the white plume on her hat bob haughtily. "Let's." She held her head up as grandly as if she were about to be presented to Queen Victoria, and the two marched grandly through the crowd. Clutching their psalm books, the temperance women fell away from them.

"Don't you fear for the state of your soul?" screeched the tall hatchet-faced woman, when they reached the double doors.

Jessie speared her with a glare. "Don't you fear for *yours?*"

Leaving the woman spluttering, they stepped into the cool dimness.

As their eyes adjusted to the dimness, they saw Martin Cordwainer sitting on the piano stool with his cuffs and collar hanging askew, grimly flexing his fingers.

"The rheumatism is definitely coming on strong today," he muttered to himself. "I shall have to dose myself with the appropriate medicine."

"Isn't it a little early in the day for that, Martin?" Jessie asked.

The piano player laughed. "Since the sun never sets on the British Empire," he said, "it seems a fair bet that it's over the yardarm, somewhere in the Queen's dominion."

"Where's Ki?"

The Englishman gave his tawny head a slight shake, blinked his eyes, and looked hard at her. "That's a fair question, Miss Starbuck," he said carefully, "considering that I now recollect that he went off with that baron of yours, not so very long ago."

"But why? I told him to stay here. It's not like him to go wandering off."

"The baron told him you'd been hurt and were asking for him," Cordwainer said. "and I should mention at this juncture how pleased I am to see you in apparently perfect health. In any event, upon hearing that, your man took off straight away."

Jessie turned to stare up at David Coulter in horror. As she did so, pieces were falling into place in her head with an almost audible sound, like the tumblers of a lock.

★

Chapter 14

When they had gone four blocks from the Liberty, Ki turned a puzzled frown to the baron, who was walking beside him with ground-devouring strides of his long slim legs.

"I do not understand," Ki said.

"Why, what is the matter?" the young Prussian asked.

"Miss Starbuck was going to see Police Chief Coates. Yet we are walking away from the center of town. Why would she have come this way?"

The baron gave an easy shrug. "Perhaps she was carried this way after her mishap."

Ki stopped. "Why would she not be taken back to the Liberty, then?" He felt the sudden conviction of error rising in his throat like bile. "I must go back."

The baron smiled a bittersweet smile. "I'm afraid that will not be possible, my friend."

Without hesitation, Ki spun. Half a dozen rough-dressed men were approaching from the rear. Several carried clubs. Seeing him turn, they spread out and approached in a semi-circle of gap-toothed grins.

I should have sensed them, he knew. He had allowed

118

himself to worry about Jessie's safety, allowed that to distract him. His employer's welfare was his paramount duty, of course, but he knew his preoccupation had gone beyond that; *giri* was shading into *ninjo*. He had allowed himself to be blinkered like a horse—and before that, to be tricked.

He picked out the smallest of the half-dozen who had been following him, a bandy-legged man with a red bandanna knotted around his dirty throat darted at him. Duty required that Ki flee, do what he could to win clear and find his employer. The samurai he had been trained to be would have experienced a conflict between his duty, which required him to run, and his honor, which demanded he stand and fight. Fortunately, the *ninja* he really was felt no such qualms.

Ki discounted the possibility that the baron would shoot him in the back. Had Pappenheim wanted him dead, the men shadowing him would have been carrying shotguns, not sticks.

Bandy-legs carried a piece of planking. As Ki charged him his eyes widened, and he threw the board up defensively before his face. Ki broke it with a downward knife-hand, smashed the man's mouth to red ruin with a straight punch from the other hand. The bandy-legged man sat down hard.

Ki tried to flash past him. Another board cracked across the back of his head from behind, driving him to his knees in the rutted street as sparks fountained behind his eyes.

A boot that seemed made of lead caught him in the ribs. He fell onto his side. The man who had kicked him showed him a grin with a gold tooth in the middle, and raised a boot to stomp him.

Ki rolled toward him, brought his leg scything around in a sweep that caught the gold-toothed man behind the heel of his planted leg, and dumped him to the ground with a thud.

Instantly Ki was on his feet, trying to sprint free. A board swung horizontally toward his face from the left. He whipped his left fist up in a block. The board shattered across his forearm.

119

A weight landed on his back. Strong arms tried to drag his arms down to his sides. He staggered three steps, went to one knee. Jackknifing his body forward, he threw the man who had jumped on him over his head.

Hands seized his arms from either side. He was dragged upright. He had a solution for that, too: sag toward one, to draw him off-balance, then throw his weight the other way and cave the man's ribs in with a side-kick, and finally turn on the man who held his other arm.

Instead he sensed a blur of motion from his right. A foot crashed against the side of his face.

The world cartwheeled around him. His knees buckled. Suspended between the two assailants, he raised his head.

A man stood before him, dressed all in black. He was tall and spare and pale, with curly black hair and sideburns that traveled down almost to the end of his lantern jaw. He gazed down at Ki with deep-set dark eyes and smiled.

"Herr Ki," came the baron's voice from behind, calm and conversational. "Permit me to introduce my man, LeClerc."

Ki started to lunge to his feet. The tall man's right foot lashed out and caught him in the pit of his stomach.

"Let him go," the man in black said in a thick accent.

The two released Ki's arms. Ki sprang upright. LeClerc was already cocking his right leg for another kick. Ki tried to block it, but the blow to the face and the kick in the gut had slowed his reactions ever so slightly.

It was enough. The tall man was fast as a striking sidewinder. His foot whipped past Ki's guard and into his solar plexus.

Ki doubled. LeClerc performed a little hop, caught Ki under the chin with a rising kick that stood him straight up. The tall man landed, brought his straightened right leg up and around.

Ki tried to raise his hands to block, but they had become vast as pillows and heavy as stone. He could do no more than watch through blurred eyes as the tall man's foot grew huge in his vision.

Then all he saw was blackness.

120

•   •   •

"I can't believe how foolish I've been," Jessie said.

"You really think your young friend the baron has played you false?" asked Coulter, who had his coat off and leaned with one elbow on the bar, sipping beer from a glass mug. They were alone in the saloon's main room—as alone as they could be with the voices of the psalm-singers outside beating against the boarded-over windows like hail. By contrast to the muggy slamming heat on the street outside, the saloon had seemed cool. Now it felt stifling.

Jessie sighed, made a face. "I'm sure of it. Why else would he lure Ki off with a phony story of how I was hurt?"

She sighed. "Besides, now I'm beginning to ask questions I should have been asking myself all along. Such as, who were those masked men who accosted me on the way back from Sister Angela's camp? And how was it, really, that the dashing young baron happened along at precisely the right moment?"

She sank into a chair. She heard the heels of Coulter's shoes thump gently on the floorboards behind her, felt his hands begin to knead her shoulders where they met her neck. His hands were surprisingly strong. She did not pull away from their touch.

"If it's any consolation, I suspect you're not the first to be taken in by Pappenheim," Coulter said. "He's a very plausible young man."

"I wonder why he's doing this."

"No way to tell at this point, and there's no point in speculating."

"You're right, I suppose." She shook her head. "I still feel as if we should do something for Ki."

"But what can we do? We don't have any idea where he is. If you leave here, all you do is make yourself a target, which won't do Ki any good. Besides," the publisher gave a soft chuckle, "your man Ki seems quite capable of taking care of himself, from what I've seen."

She smiled, reached back to caress one of his hands.

121

"You're right. Ki has a way of landing on his feet. But I can't help worrying."

"We might have worries much closer to home before long," Coulter said. "I suspect they wouldn't have taken Ki if they weren't getting ready to act."

She nodded. Warmth flowed through her body, downward from the strong and confident touch of his hands. She was concerned for Ki, but she knew full well that Coulter was right, there was nothing to be done for him now. And perhaps her fear was whetting the appetite she felt rising within her. She turned her face and kissed Coulter's right hand.

"Miss Starbuck," a deep male voice said from the saloon door.

Torch flames danced, defying the first few drops of rain spattering down from a bullet-colored sky. To the west the sun was melting into the horizon in an angry explosion of color, red and orange and yellow, beneath a band of cloud the colors of a bruise.

"The time has come!" Sister Angela declared from the dais. It was three feet high and fifteen square, which was knocked apart and bundled up whenever the Army shifted camp, along with Sister Angela's pavilion and furniture, to be reassembled when a new target for salvation was reached. The Temperance Army rumbled and surged around the platform like surf on a stormy sea.

"Amen!" cried the crowd. The faithful knew something great was about to happen. It charged the air with electricity, like the storm rolling in from the east.

"We have come to this fair city with love and faith in our hearts, to close down that devil's den known as the Liberty," the sister declared, her blue eyes blazing. "But its proprietress has defied the will of the Lord. Now it's time to show her, the Lord will not be denied!"

"Amen!" her soldiers cried again.

"I say unto you, this very night shall we march as did the forces of Joshua upon the ramparts of Jericho. And the walls of the Liberty shall be trampled beneath our feet, and

122

that devil's brew which it dispenses will mingle with God's cleansing rains in the gutters of Center City!"

A man leapt to the top of an upended cracker barrel and waved his hat in the air. "Hallelujah!" he cried.

"I go now to my tent to meditate and pray, and strengthen myself for the coming confrontation," the sister said, ignoring a drop of rain that struck her cheek and exploded in a fine spray. Other droplets made dark spots on the yellow satin dress she wore. "I can only beseech the Lord to open the heart of the woman known as Jessica Starbuck, so that no harm may come to any. But whatever befalls, brothers and sisters, tonight without question God's will shall be done in Center City!"

To ecstatic cries of "Praise the Lord!" and "Hallelujah," Sister Angela marched from the platform, her splendid blond head held high.

Inside her large tent the evangelist faced the three men who awaited her there. "Where is the captive?" she asked them.

Twisting the brim of his bowler, Dan Brokaw said, "You needn't trouble yourself with the likes of him, dear sister. He'll trouble you no more."

"I want to see him."

"Are you sure that's wise, Fräulein?" the baron von Pappenheim asked solicitously. "After all, he was on his way here to assassinate you when he was intercepted by my faithful LeClerc." The third and largest man in the room performed a perfunctory bow at mention of his name.

The sister looked skeptically at the baron. "The Lord works in mysterious ways," she said, "and He has sent you to me, so I don't suppose I should examine your case too strongly, Baron. All the same, you seem too smooth for me by half."

The young nobleman stiffened. Then he clicked his heels and bowed himself. "I wish only to serve you, Fräulein," he said. "If I have given offense—"

"It isn't I, but the will of the Lord, that needs to be served here," she said coolly. "The only way you will offend me as if you go on arguing about my simple request. I want to see Miss Starbuck's employee, and I want to see him now."

Brokaw glanced nervously at Pappenheim. "The baron knows of this man through, through contacts," he said. His voice turned to a stammer when she turned her furious blue glare upon him. "I—he assures me the man is a master assassin, t-trained in all manner of devilish Oriental arts!"

"Are you *arguing* with me, Danny?" the evangelist demanded in a dangerous tone.

"No—never. But s-still—"

"There, there, Danny," Sister Angela said in a softer tone. She stepped forward, caressed him lightly on the cheek. He squeezed his eyes briefly shut, as if anticipating a slap. "I'm sorry I spoke so crisply to you. I know you're only trying to look out for me. But the Lord watches out for me. You ought to know that."

He swallowed, nodded wordlessly. She stepped back. "I'm retiring to my chamber to fortify my spirit with prayer, gentlemen," she said sweetly. "I'm certain I can rely upon you to have the prisoner delivered to me in not above five minutes, can't I?"

"Sister Angela."

She raised her blond head from the table beside which she knelt, hands clasped to her sizable bosom. Ki stood between two larger men, black hair hanging in his sloe eyes and his arms bound behind his back.

"Mr. Brokaw said you wanted to see this one," said the man on the right, who was tall and blond, with a not un-handsome young face marred mainly by a slack moist-lipped mouth. He wore a red bandanna around his neck, which Sister Angela saw was none too clean. Like Ki's other escort, he wore a pair of heavy revolvers in a well-worn gunbelt at his hip.

Sister Angela frowned, and her lips tightened. She disapproved of her followers going about armed; they were armored in the knowledge that they were soldiers of the Lord, after all. She understood that this was probably another of

Danny's precautions; he really was as much a mother to her as a brother, and out of that concern sometimes did things which might make another wonder if his faith in the Lord had wavered. She did not recognize either of the gunmen. Probably they were new men, recruited out of Center City, and did not know about her aversion to weapons. She would have a few words with Danny, ask him to speak with them about it. *Later.*

"Thank you, gentlemen," she said.

"Um, are you sure we had oughta leave you alone with this here varmint, ma'am?" asked the other man. He was shorter, darker, and a few years older than the other, with a thick neck and stubbled cheeks. "He's a desperado, sure."

Definitely new men, Sister Angela thought. "What are your names, gentlemen," she asked, "if you'd be so kind as to enlighten me? I'm afraid you're not familiar to me."

"I'm Billy Dill," the blond young man said. "This here's the Tucumcari Kid."

"Very well, Mr. Dill and Mr., ah, Kid. You are no doubt new to the Temperance Army. Still, you shall soon learn that I am the Lord's humble servant, and as such enjoy His complete protection. You may withdraw now."

The Tucumcari Kid started to say something. Dill nudged him in the ribs and he shut his mouth. The loose-mouthed blond man shoved Ki roughly forward, and the two turned and went out.

Ki raised his head to glare at Sister Angela. She met his intense black gaze without flinching.

"Follow me," she said. She turned away, walked through a flap of canvas into a room deeper still within the outsized tent.

He was alone. He drew in a deep breath through his nose, expelled in from his mouth, breathing from the diaphragm. He might well make a break for it now—except that the tent was doubtless ringed by hired gunmen like Dill and the Tucumcari Kid. This extravagant *gaijin* woman might believe those two were moved by the spirit of her temperance crusade. Ki, who had faced their like a hundred times, knew

125

better: they were killers, moved only by the clink of hard yellow gold in their palms.

Ki was a warrior, and in his sense of duty to Jessie at least, a true samurai. But his mother's people had an expression: "any dog can die in a ditch". His life was not truly his; he might lay it down unthinkingly to preserve the life of his employer, but it would be gross dereliction to throw it away in a hopeless bid for escape.

Besides, something was happening here, something he did not understand. Something his warrior's instincts told him might be very significant indeed. So he would bide his time, and see what the future brought.

Sister Angela was standing by an incongruous brass bed when he stepped through the curtain. Her hair glowed like fine silk in the light of a kerosene lamp.

"Come forward, Mr. Ki," she said.

He took two steps and came to a halt four feet from her. He smelled the clean well-soaped scent of her. Though she had the smell of one who ate a lot of red meat instead of fish, that odor no longer troubled him, after so many years among Americans.

"Do you believe in God, Mr. Ki?"

Like any good *ninja,* Ki had been brought up a Buddhist. Like any good Japanese, he had also been brought up honoring the *kami* of the native Shinto pantheon, and was additionally willing to be open to the possible validity of other collections of gods and spirits as well. This did not seem the time to try to explain the ins and outs of his beliefs in any detail—especially since he hadn't really codified them himself.

"I believe there is a force beyond man," he said evenly, "and I believe our actions are judged."

Sister Angela smiled. "So they are, Mr. Ki, and while my stricter brothers in the Lord might disagree, I'd call you a believing man," she said "Turn around."

Feeling no immediate presentiment of danger, and wondering just what she was up to, Ki complied. He felt the kiss of steel cool against his wrists, felt a momentary flash

126

of self-anger. She had a knife, and he had made a mistake in believing he was safe, however momentarily. . . .

The rough ropes fell away from his wrists. He raised his hands and began to try to massage the blood back into them. They felt as if he were wearing gloves studded with inward-pointing needles.

"You may turn back around, Mr. Ki."

He did so, in time to see her laying a hunting knife with a six-inch blade on a table next to the bed. "Do you also believe in Providence?" she asked. There was a curious glitter in her eyes.

"I believe in the Wheel of Karma."

Her fingers were busy at the bodice of her dress. "You must tell me about it someday," she said in an oddly throaty voice. "I knew from the moment that I laid eyes upon you that we were fated to come together."

"I am your prisoner," Ki said in a flat voice.

She smiled. "No you're not," she said quietly. She let the dress fall to the muted rose-patterned carpet which floored the tent. Beneath it she was nude.

"You're not that at all." She held her arms out to him.

★

Chapter 15

A pair of men stood in the double doors, silhouetted against the twilight. The setting sun splashed lemon-colored light over the fronts of the buildings across Central. David Coulter's right hand slipped from Jessie's shoulder and into the right pocket of his linen coat.

It occurred to Jessie that that pocket had been hanging a mite heavy this afternoon. Carrying a pistol in one's pocket was far from uncommon, but she hadn't known David to do it. This was definitely a day of surprises.

"May I help you, gentlemen?" she asked, rising. Both were tall and broad-shouldered in dusters and broad-brimmed hats. The wider one had a bulky jute sack slung over his back.

"Miss Starbuck?" that one asked. His voice was a rich baritone, and Jessie realized with a touch of surprise that he was black.

"Yes."

The man with the bag removed his hat. His head was balding. His eyes were set deep in a handsome, heavy-jawed face.

128

"I'm Dolphus Jefferson," he said. "I'm Andy's uncle. This here's his brother, Tyrone."

He nudged the man standing next to him. Hastily that one took off his hat. He was a youngster, with a skinny neck and prominent Adam's apple. Jessie realized he only looked bulky by reason of the coat.

"Pleased to meet you, Miss," said Tyrone.

"Did Andy get home all right?" Coulter asked.

Tyrone's eyes flicked aside to his uncle. Dolphus Jefferson nodded. "Yes he did, Mr. Coulter," the young man said. "We got him hid away safe now, where no one's gonna find him."

"I'm glad to hear that," the publisher said. He took his hand out of his pocket and stood easy.

Rain had begun to tap on the planks nailed over the windows, and the saloon filled with its thick, woody smell. The psalm-singers outside faltered, but carried on bravely.

"We appreciate what you did for Andy, Mr. Coulter," Dolphus Jefferson said. "I can't say I approve of everything you've seen fit to print in your paper, being a God-fearing man, but I reckon you got a right to publish what you please. We're right beholden to you. You too, Miss Starbuck, for what your man did."

"Would you gentlemen care for a drink?" Jessie asked. She gestured at the bar, which was currently unmanned. "We weren't expecting many customers, what with our friendly serenaders outside."

"You sure won't be gettin' many, ma'am," Tyrone said. "Word's all over town. Temperance Army fixin' to clean y'all out for good and all tonight!"

Jessie sucked in her breath. She glanced at David, who set his jaw.

"I thank you for coming by, gentlemen," Jessie said. "But I reckon you'd best move on before the trouble starts."

Tyrone blinked, looked to his uncle. "We didn't drop by just to thank you with words, Miss," Jefferson said. He lowered the bag from his shoulder. It made an unmistakable metallic clump when it hit the floor that brought Jessie's eyes wide.

"We come to help out," Tyrone said, eyes bright.

"With your permission," Dolphus said, "we'll be staying." He took a Peacemaker in a gunbelt and a double-barreled shotgun from the sack, and handed both to his nephew.

"Aren't you . . ." She hesitated. She would not insult these men by using the word *afraid*. " . . . concerned about what Chief Coates might do?"

Tyrone had taken a box of shotgun shells from the sack, plopped it on the table, and broken open the double gun to stuff a couple of fat wax-paper cartridges into the breech. He showed her horsy white teeth.

"Ain't afeerd of *him*."

"Chief Coates likes to back a winning mount, Miss Starbuck," Dolphus Jefferson said. He withdrew a Sharps carbine from the sack, all gleaming wood and bright-polished brass, and laid it on the table. "If we stand off these temperance boomers, he won't say a word but to come 'round when the smoke clears and take credit for it all."

"And if we don't?" Jessie asked.

Dolphus showed her a shrug and a lopsided smile.

She took a deep breath. "Since you both know what you're getting into . . . welcome, and I thank you."

A thump of boot heels sounded on the stoop. Jessie looked past the two black men, to see a lopsided shadow looming in the door.

"Mr. McAllister," she said, as the one-armed, red-bearded stable owner came clomping in. "And what's this? Mr. Sylvester?" The owner of the town millinery, a fussy portly man with a sleek little moustache, had followed the stable owner in.

"I've grown unused to so much custom in one afternoon," Jessie said.

"We did not come to drink, Miss Starbuck," Sylvester said.

"Though I wouldn't say no to a drop of whiskey," McAllister added. "We're here to give a hand."

"My heartfelt thanks, Mr. McAllister," Jessie said, "but

understand, things are likely to get pretty hot in this vicinity."

"So we hear," said McAllister.

"We came prepared," added Sylvester. He reached into the pocket of his black coat and produced a rimfire Colt House pistol, which resembled a derringer with a fat cylinder. He waved it for everyone to see. Coulter and Dolphus Jefferson dodged to keep the little weapon from coming to bear on them.

Jessie looked hard at the little millinery store owner. His wife, a silver-haired women with a formidable bosom and two chins, had snubbed Jessie since the day of her arrival. "Are you sure you want to do this, Mr. Sylvester?"

He nodded vigorously, still brandishing the House pistol. "It's a disgrace, the way these Temperance Army ruffians think they can march in and just take over a town. We intend to show them we've had enough."

"There were plenty of folks agreed with what they had to say at first," McAllister said in his heavy, gravelly voice. "But we don't cotton to the midnight shooting and the beating and killing and . . . other stuff."

Jessie stuffed down a wild impulse to laugh like a loon at the mores of the day, which made it acceptable for the big stableman to speak to Jessie of violent deeds, but unable to mention rape.

"Would your wife approve, Mr. Sylvester?" she asked.

He blinked, and for a moment indecisiveness turned his face to custard pudding. McAllister gave him a bearlike scowl.

"I don't need her permission to act like a man," the store owner said crisply. "Though she's as outraged as I am by the excesses of this Sister Angela."

Got a look at her décolletage, more like, Jessie thought. She said no more.

"My nephew and me are here to help out, too," said Dolphus Jefferson, strapping a pair of Navy Colts around his waist. By the cartridges stuck through loops in the belt, the weapons had clearly been bored-out so that they were no longer cap-and-ball, but fired modern metal-cased

131

ammunition instead. He put his hands on his hips and looked square at the newcomers. "Does that make you any problems, gentlemen?"

"I allus reckoned," McAllister growled, "that any man's willing to stand up on his hind legs and fight for what he believes in is a good enough man for me."

Sylvester looked a little dubious, but said, "Yes. Yes, of course."

Without making a show of it, David Coulter had walked to his side. Now he gently pushed the barrel of the little Colt up with the back of one hand.

"If you'd just stash that away, Mr. Sylvester," he said, "perhaps Miss Starbuck could find a nice spare shotgun for you to use."

"Oh, my *Lord!*" The woman's voice soared like a bird, the words—and passion—unmistakable even through two walls of heavy canvas. "Halle*lu*jah!"

A brisk rain had begun to beat upon the pavilion. It and the noise the crowd—too keyed up by the words of Sister Angela and a succession of other orators to be discouraged by the increasing downpour—was making might be enough to keep the Temperance Army from hearing all too clearly what its commander and guiding light was up to. Dan Brokaw took his handkerchief from the breast pocket of his brown suit and mopped his wide forehead, which had lost much of its color.

"We're ruined," he said to the baron in a hoarse whisper. "This devastates all our planning."

"Compose yourself," the baron said, his fine face set in an expression of mixed amusement and contempt. "It devastates our plans not at all—whatever damage it may wreak to your own agenda."

"And what do you mean by that?" Brokaw snapped.

"You have entertained hopes of your own dalliance with our fair Sister Angela, have you not?"

Eyes terrible, Brokaw took a step forward. LeClerc growled low in his throat.

132

"Come now, Herr Brokaw," Pappenheim said. "You think to do me harm, with my faithful LeClerc on hand? Not to say that I am at all inconsiderable."

Still scowling, Brokaw gestured at the pair of gunslingers, who were shifting their weight and licking their lips at the sounds coming from the back of the pavilion. "What about them? I hired them?"

"And I pay them." He grinned. "So whom do you think they will obey? Would you care to place a wager?"

Billy Dill and his partner traded looks and grins. "Reckon that's about the way she stands," the Tucumcari Kid said.

Dan Brokaw let all the air out of him. His outsized head sank toward his upright collar.

"Now then," Pappenheim said. "Now that you have regained control of yourself, perhaps you can see how this situation works precisely to our advantage."

"Ohhh, *God!*" Sister Angela voice cried.

Brokaw moistened his lips. "Tell me," he croaked. "Our spies say some townies have actually turned up to help the Starbuck woman defend her place. Dozens of weak sisters are nervous and ready to bolt because of the rumors over what happened to that slut of a dancing girl; they don't reckon such things are Godly, the fools. And now this!"

"It is simplicity itself," the baron said. "Sister Angela has been asking pointed questions about the Starbuck woman's accusations, nicht wahr? As you yourself observed, our strength is undermined by an epidemic of weak wills; and to truly become unstoppable, the Temperance Army needs a martyr."

He smiled. "Therefore: shortly it will be revealed to the faithful that Jessica Starbuck's yellow-skinned servant has raped and murdered the beloved Sister. The Temperance Army will rise up in righteous wrath, and in their avenging fury will roll over the Liberty and its defenders and crush all utterly—including the inconvenient Miss Starbuck. And from there . . ."

A shrug. "Perhaps the tide will roll on across Kansas, and indeed all America. The only question will be, shall we enjoy a smashing local victory, or total victory?"

"Oh Lord," Sister Angela's muffled voice moaned. "Good Lord, *please*."

A violent shudder wracked Brokaw's slight frame, like a terrier shaking a rat. "For God's sake, then, let's get on with it."

"No," the baron said. "We shall wait. It would be unchivalrous to interrupt, don't you think?"

★

Chapter 16

The rain had started to fall in earnest on Center City. The drops fell with such fury that in bursting on the flat roof of the Liberty they created a shin-high mist.

Clutching a coat about her shoulders, Jessie yelled, "Will you be all right up here?"

Dolphus Jefferson nodded, cascading rain off his broad-brimmed hat. "Yes, ma'am," he said. "Man who works the land learns not to mind a little rain."

Bern McAllister peered through a crack in the Liberty's false front, which rose a story above the roof on the Central side. He carried a Winchester carbine. Jessie wondered how well he could operate it with one arm, but he handled it with the easy confidence of experience. "Least them confounded psalm-singers have gone home."

It was true. Central and Sullivan were empty, except for the rainwater pooling in ruts.

"Maybe the rest of the Temperance Army will get the same idea," Jessie said. Her hair was hanging around her face, limp as a dead wet animal. It was chill and miserable up here, as if this were an entirely different season from the

135

thumping heat of day. David Coulter stood behind her, and she drew warmth from his presence.

Jefferson and McAllister traded looks. "Don't reckon that's any too likely, Miss," rumbled the stable owner. "There's been some powerful harsh talk going on out at the Temperance camp. And the word is they mean to settle this tonight."

"Don't worry 'bout a thing, ma'am. We'll keep a good watch up here." Dolphus Jefferson said.

"What about your nephew?" Jessie asked. The younger Jefferson was down in the main room, keeping watch with Mr. Sylvester. "He seems a bit eager."

"He'll be all right, ma'am," the farmer said. "It's mostly that he's young."

He slapped the receiver of his Sharps, which he had wrapped in waxed paper and stuffed back in the jute sack for protection against the wet. "Frederick Douglass says the two things which will keep the black man free are the ballot box and the cartridge box. We know how to take care of ourselves."

"Don't just stand there," Jessie said to David Coulter, who stood framed in the doorway of her second-floor bedroom. "You're soaked through to the skin. Come ahead on in. Ki doesn't have much by way of clothes, but maybe we can scare up something from his room to fit you."

The lanky blond publisher hesitated. "I hate to impose. And I'm afraid his things would be a bit short for me."

"Suit yourself," she said. She knew he was admiring the way the wet molded her white shirt to her full breasts and made it sheer. She caught the ends of her hair, turned copper-brown by the rain, wrung water from it into a washtub. "Would you mind helping me towel this dry?"

"Not at all." Coulter came forward, picked up a big white towel from the bed, began to knead Jessie's hair dry with those surprisingly powerful hands. Jessie sat on the edge of the bed to facilitate the work.

When her hair was somewhat dry she reached up and

caught him by one hand, kissed the back of it. "Seems to me this is the point where we got interrupted," Jessie said in a husky voice. "Or am I being too forward? I'd hate to scare you off."

Coulter chuckled low in his throat. "There are things in this world I'm scared of," he admitted, "but a beautiful woman isn't one of them. Even one who goes ahead and speaks her mind."

"Is that so?" she asked, green eyes half-lidded.

He bent and kissed her. She opened her mouth, accepted his tongue, caressed it hungrily with hers.

He was beside her on the bed, then, one hand cupping her right breast, catching a fabric-covered nipple between thumb and forefinger and rolling it gently to and fro. The slight rasp of the shirt material on her sensitive flesh made Jessie's breath catch in her throat. She began to fumble at the buttons of his fly.

His own free hand made play with the buttons of her jeans. She felt air spill in, cool across her lower belly, as the jeans opened, and then his hand was sweet fire sliding down the rough patch of her pubic fur, between her thighs. She gasped as he slid a finger up inside her.

When she broke the seal of their lips he dropped his head to the base of her throat, began to nibble at her while he tore her shirt wide open. Buttons flew, clattered off the shutters, and rolled across the floor. Her breasts came free, pink nipples taut, as much for the touch of cool air as for the excitement mounting within her.

Continuing to stroke his finger in and out of her, he laved her breasts with his tongue. He engulfed a pink nipple with his mouth. She cried out as he nipped it, ever so gently. Then he fastened his lips around it and flicked the tip with his tongue till she grabbed the hair at the back of his head and moaned.

He relinquished her nipple, left it quivering and wet, slid his lips down the flat dome of her belly. At the same time he began to tug her jeans downward. The wet denim clung; she kicked her boots off and they went skittering across the

137

room, then she lay back, arched her body in a bow with only her shoulders and the backs of her knees in contact with the bed, and skinned the jeans down her long, shapely shanks.

She screamed, then, as he buried her face in her, delving his tongue deep into her sex, dragging it excruciatingly upwards from the depths of her to tease at the tiny pink pearl of ultra-sensitive flesh nestled at the juncture of her lips.

She came, her orgasm sudden and shattering as a thunderbolt. One hand clutched at the bedclothes by her head while the other grabbed the back of his head and held him while she writhed against him, calling out in wordless ecstasy.

When the spasm passed she collapsed, feeling wrung-out as a bar rag. She pushed him gently away. He smiled up at her, his long handsome face framed by thighs which seemed to quiver like the surface of a pool into which a pebble had just been dropped.

"Come on," she said, tugging at his shirt. "Take me." Coulter grinned, reared back, unbuttoned his shirt, took it off, and tossed it aside, then stepped out of his trousers. He was rigidly erect, ready for her.

He put a knee on the bed beside her, lay down, and rolled on his back. With a hungry growl from the base of her throat she rolled atop him, covering his mouth with hers. For a time they lay that way, flesh to flesh, her breasts flattened against the flat muscles of his chest, her mouth locked to his, his sex throbbing against her furry mound like a heated iron bar.

When she could stand it no longer she broke the kiss and stood up on her knees, straddling him like a horse. She reached down to position his rigid sex, then eased herself down upon it. She gasped when she felt the contact between its engorged head and her, then threw back her head and cried out as she impaled herself upon him.

There was no finesse to their coupling. She fell forward onto him, devouring his mouth while his hands mauled her breasts, pumping her rump up and down so that his hardness pistoned in and out of her with locomotive force. He reached one hand to grab a handful of her round-muscled ass, and his heels were digging deep into the lumpy old mattress for traction, and his own body was arching backward like a bow, raising her clean off the bed as they spent themselves, their cries of passion muffled by each other's mouths.

At last, their lust momentarily sated, Jessie collapsed on top of David. They lay for a time, gently caressing each other, as he gradually grew soft within her.

"Now I know you think I'm forward," Jessie said hoarsely.

He smiled. Somewhere along the way his glasses had vanished. She hoped they hadn't gotten broken.

"Not at all," he said. "I think you're just right."

She kissed him on the nose and rolled off him. Cradling her head on his outflung arm, she studied his profile.

"You weren't kidding about fighting those men to help Andy, were you?" she asked. He shook his head. "I have a feeling I've got some things to learn about you."

"I'm not being mysterious on purpose," he said. As the rain tapped on the shuttered windows with increasingly impatient fingers, he told her the story he had told Ki.

"Jethro Coulter was your father?" she asked when he was done. He nodded. "I *knew* your name sounded familiar! My father knew Jethro Coulter. He used to do business with him, off in the Spice Islands."

"I know. I even met him once, before I got shipwrecked. A most impressive man."

"That he was." She ran her fingertip through the sparse brown thatch on his chest and picked herself up on one elbow. "Tell me one thing."

"Anything."

"Why weren't you fighting to defend your press, that day Ki and I met you?"

He shrugged. "I've seen enough violence in my time," he said. "More than enough. They're my neighbors, after all, people I have to live among. I figured there were too many of them to take on unless I was prepared to do something pretty immediate and drastic to somebody, to catch the attention of the rest."

He grabbed her hand, brought it to his lips, kissed it. "Then when you folks made your timely arrival, Ki made brisk enough work of them that there really wasn't much for me to do. I apologize, by the way; it's never my intent to let other people do my fighting for me."

"Ki certainly didn't mind the exercise," she said. "But why did you fight the mob that attacked Andy?"

He looked at her. "I got mad," he said.

Sister Angela was having the religious experience of her life. Buck naked on all fours, with her blond hair spilling like honey from a jar across her creamy white shoulders, her big cherry-tipped breasts swinging rhythmically below her ribs as Ki piled into her from behind, she was experiencing sensations she had never before even dreamed of.

Ki stood on his knees on her big feather bed with the four polished brass posts. Sometimes he held her narrow waist, sometimes he grabbed great handfuls of the firm flesh of her rump and squeezed it between his powerful fingers. Every now and then, as he shook the sweat from his eyes the corner of his vision caught on the glitter of kerosene lamplight on the naked blade of the hunting knife on the nightstand.

At the moment there didn't seem much use for it.

He had already made her come three times, with fingers and tongue and his own rigid manhood. Now he was playing her like an exotic musical instrument, building her toward a shattering crescendo. He increased the tempo of his strokes, bit by bit. As her gasps began to come closer together and her blond head began to bob up and down, he leaned forward, cupped her large luscious breasts in his hard palms, and drew her upright onto her knees.

She screamed, began to writhe and toss her head of glorious curls. The firm cheeks of her ass were pressed against his crotch.

He felt the tension build inside her. He redoubled the

fury of his assault, dropped one hand to her sex, found her clitoris with his index finger, and began to swirl it around and around as he drove himself savagely up and down inside her.

She shrieked to bulge the canvas walls against the relentless pressure of the rain. At some dim remove of his consciousness he marveled that her outcries didn't bring the whole Temperance Army storming in on them. And then he felt the pressure build unbearably within his own loins, and he let himself go, so that they scaled the summit together, became for a moment one flesh, one entity locked in the embrace of unalloyed pleasure.

They fell together onto the bed. She squirmed around to face him, hugged him to her breasts, and kissed him on the cheek.

"I knew you'd never hurt me," she said. With warrior discipline Ki kept his eyes from flicking aside to the knife on the nightstand. He was not set up to feel guilt, but he would regret if he had to press the tip of that knife under the sleek line of Sister Angela's jaw and take her for a hostage. He would regret it—but he would do it, if that were what it took to get him away from here and back to Jessie's side before the Temperance Army attacked.

The lovely nude evangelist went on in a breathless rush. "The Lord provides for me. He sent you here, I know it— sent you to bring me a whole new revelation, to open my eyes to vistas I've never seen before!"

Ki smiled. Here was something he could work with. "Perhaps that is so, my child," he said, reaching to caress her cheek. "There are more ways of showing devotion than even you have known."

"Oh, I *know*," she breathed. To demonstrate her newfound knowledge she reached down, took hold of his half-deflated masculinity, and gave it an affectionate squeeze.

Despite his recent release, he responded, felt himself begin to stiffen again at once. He understood well how the presence of danger whetted the appetites. "Angela," he said, "wait. You must consider—"

"I know what I *want* to consider," she purred, steering his semi-stiff manhood toward her moist-lipped open mouth.

The canvas flap that separated her bedroom from her sitting room flew open. Three men crowded into the bedchamber. All had six-guns holstered at their waists. Two held lengths of rope in their hands. The third held a Winchester leveled from the hip at the naked evangelist and her half-Japanese lover.

★

Chapter 17

"Hey, Sam," said one of the men with the ropes, "Looky what we got here."

"Yow*ie*," said the other, licking his lips. "Be a pure shame to let a purty little tail like that go to waste."

The man with the rifle moistened his own lips, which were surrounded by a half-day's stubble of dark beard. "Yeah," he said. "But we got our orders from Brokaw: choke the bitch and then shoot the Chink."

Sister Angela uttered a gasp of outrage and crammed the back of one hand in her mouth. "But Sam," the first man with the rope said in a wheedling voice, "if we keep it nice and quiet, whose gonna know what we did afore we did her in?"

"Billy Ray, you know we ain't got time to go messin'—"

Quick as a prairie rattler, Ki snatched the knife from the bedside table and threw it into the rifleman's right eye. It sank to the hilt in the socket. He dropped the Winchester, clapped a hand to his blood-gushing face, and collapsed.

The men with the ropes stood staring openmouthed. Ki

sprang off the bed in a tigerish rush. He lifted Billy Ray's bootheels an inch off the carpet with an instep kick to the family jewels, and as the desperado came back down to earth, Ki plucked the rope from his fingers, slipped behind him, and took a rapid turn of it around his dirty neck.

The third man dropped his rope and clawed his sidearm out of its holster. As its barrel came up, Ki's foot lashed out and knocked the weapon spinning from the gunslinger's hand.

The man spat a curse and aimed a haymaker for Ki's head. Ki pivoted, dragging his captive around by the throat. The hired gunman's fist thudded against his partner's face. The man quit clawing at the rope digging into his neck and sagged.

"Ow! Shit! My hand!" The gunman jerked back, shaking his damaged hand. Ki brought his right foot whipping up and around and slammed a roundhouse kick against the side of his head. His eyes rolled up and he fell.

The man Ki still held in an improvised noose had come out of his stunned state and was beginning to struggle feebly. Ki put his knee in the small of his back, yanked the rope cruelly tight around his throat, and tied it off. Then he pushed the man face-first down upon the rose-patterned carpet, to writhe and slowly strangle.

"Those men meant to *kill* me," Sister Angela said, voice throbbing with disbelief. "Did you hear? Dan Brokaw, that traitor."

Ki had found his pants, lying by one wall of the tent. Holding them draped over his arm, he planted his bare foot on the cheek of the rifleman and pulled the knife out of his eye socket. It made a sucking sound. Sister Angela retched and turned away.

Ki grabbed the naked crusader by the arm and dragged her unceremoniously off the bed. Sobbing and gagging, she tried to hold back.

"We have no time," he said. He pulled the flowered coverlet from the bed and flung it around her shoulders.

"In a moment someone will come to see what's taking them so long."

She sniffled, rubbed at her suddenly red nose with a knuckle, and nodded. Ki slashed an opening in the tent's back wall and bending down, dragged her behind him into the downpour.

"Damn, damn, *damn!*" Dan Brokaw exclaimed, voice rising until it was almost a scream. "They've gotten away! We're ruined!"

"Contain yourself," the baron said. "Not half an hour ago you were shocked by the necessity of Sister Angela's death. Now you are dismayed that she has escaped."

The face Brokaw turned toward him had gone ashen in the light of the lone kerosene lantern illuminating the evangelist's bed chamber. "Don't you see? What if the mob—if the Temperance Army finds out what's happened?" He shuddered. "They'll tear us to pieces."

The wind was flapping the raw edges of the slash Ki had made in the rear of the tent. Every now and then a spray of raindrops spattered the men crowded into the room: the former newsman, Pappenheim and his giant manservant, Billy Dill, and his sidekick. After a glance at his master, LeClerc was helping the surviving member of the trio which had burst in on Ki and Angela to his feet. One side of the man's face was already a livid bruise mask.

"They will not dare present themselves to the mob," Pappenheim said confidently. "They do not know whom they can trust. And that half-Asian mongrel will head directly for the Starbuck woman's side."

Leaning over, he picked up the dress Sister Angela had been wearing off the carpet. He tossed it to the moaning gunman Ki had kicked. "Hold this a moment."

By reflex the man caught the garment, stood blinking with it held against his chest. With a smooth motion Pappenheim snaked the Tucumcari Kid's lefthand Peacemaker from its holster and shot the bruised gunman right through the dress. A gout of his blood stained the fabric, and he fell.

"What the *hell* is going on?" Billy Dill demanded loudly. He dropped his hand to the grips of his own .44. LeClerc laid a heavy hand on his shoulder.

"I have no brief with failure," the young Prussian said, sliding the weapon back into the now sweating Kid's holster. "Make sure that message is transmitted to your surviving men."

He bent and picked up the dress yet again. "I have also fabricated a most convincing stage prop for you, Herr Brokaw."

He threw the bloodstained dress at the former journalist. Brokaw caught it and held it gingerly away from him.

"Now go forth and put our original plan into effect," the baron commanded. "LeClerc, you go and hunt down our fugitive evangelist and her combative friend."

"Do you require that they be brought back alive, Baron?" the huge French Canadian asked.

The young noble showed him a shark's smile. "Not at all, my good man. Not at all."

Head bared to the downpour, Dan Brokaw mounted the platform and waved the bloody dress above his head. The torches had long since been murdered by the rain, but kerosene lanterns hung from poles provided enough illumination to show the garment and the black-looking stain.

"Soldiers of the Temperance Army," he cried, "a terrible thing has happened! The sacred person of our beloved Sister Angela has been subjected to the vilest outrages, and she has been cruelly murdered. Behold the blood of the innocent!"

A gasp rose from the crowd. "Who done it?" a voice demanded. "Who done the wicked deed?"

"It was the Starbuck woman's Chinaman, who works with her at that den of sin, the Liberty! He has stolen our dear sister away from us."

The mob vented a single incoherent scream of grief and fury. Then, as one many-legged beast, it began to slouch toward the bridge that led across the rain-swollen Jericho toward Center City.

Thunder crashed like a cannonade. "My word," Sister Angela said in a low voice. "It certainly has gotten chilly out here." Her fingers were moving constantly about her amply endowed person, trying to seal the blanket against the rain-saturated air. It was a hopeless cause.

Ki held a finger to his lips. They were hunkered down behind a low swell of land in the driving rain, watching the last of a several hundred strong Temperance Army mob march purposefully across the bridge. There were several horsemen dotted among them; Brokaw's hired guns, he guessed, and he thought he glimpsed the high-stepping black stallion the baron favored, though distance, rain, and darkness prevented him from identifying the rider with any certainty.

Once out of immediate sight of the Temperance Army encampment, with no signs of pursuit yet showing, he had paused long enough to pull on his trousers. Since then he had kept up a grueling pace across country, paralleling the path the temperance soldiers took to the bridge. The cold and the wet troubled him not at all; he noticed them only in so much as they affected the tactical situation. He hadn't spent all that time standing naked under icy waterfalls in the Eight Islands for nothing.

The mob was carrying lanterns in lieu of the customary torches. That and the fact that their attention was fixed resolutely on Center City and retribution—Ki hadn't heard Brokaw's stirring speech to the crowd, but he was shrewd enough to guess what their enemies' actions would be once their escape was known—gave him a certain confidence that the two fugitives would not be spotted crouching half-naked in the rain.

Sister Angela sat down, without bothering to pull some blanket under her to save her well-shaped rump from contact with the cold, sodden ground. Aside from her mild remark about the temperature, she had made no complaints. Ki had permitted himself to be seduced by her both as a samurai, properly lusty, and as a *ninja,* always keen to scavenge every speck of advantage a situation might offer. But he was beginning to form a grudging respect for the lovely blond evangelist; she did not lack for spirit.

"You know," she said in a quiet conversational voice that the rain sounds quickly swallowed, "this has been a night of revelations for me. I have seen that I have been blind and willful, and have confused the Lord's wishes and desires with my own. And my eyes have been opened to that generation of serpents which I have clasped to my bosom."

The right half of that impressive bosom was peeking out the front of her blanket. As Ki glanced back a raindrop struck the tip of her nipple and exploded, bringing the pink nipple quiveringly erect in a circle of goose-bumped aureole. He was not too much the warrior to hope they both might live long enough to enjoy another erotic go-round. He no longer considered her an enemy. She was fleeing for her life every bit as much as he was.

Her next words confirmed his judgment: "I've been manipulated like a puppet. By that smooth devil the baron— and by Dan Brokaw, whom I trusted as my brother."

She leaned forward to kiss Ki's wet gleaming cheek. "I owe you much, my beautiful Chinaman. You have opened my eyes. Not to mention other parts of me."

He nodded absently. It had been years since he had resented being taken for Chinese. Few Americans outside of New York and San Francisco had so much as heard of Japan, and his engrained Japanese prejudice against mainlanders, half-contemptuous, half-awed, had long since been scoured from him by frequent contact with Chinese folk.

The bridge was clear. The curtains of rain had hidden even the glow of Temperance Army lanterns. Ki felt a sudden driving urgency. They were marching to attack the Liberty. His employer was in danger. He had to rejoin her as soon as possible, but he knew full well the two of them had to avoid contact with the mob at all costs.

"Come on," he said, rising. "We'll go to the river and approach the bridge along the bank. That way we're less likely to encounter stragglers."

She nodded and stood. Taking her hand he began to move at a rapid pace, toes splayed for purchase on the treacherous wet grass, cringing in reflex fear of discovery when a flash of lightning lit the scene. The river was full and gurgling loud enough to be heard above the downpour. He kept them a bit back from the bank itself, lest a sudden mudslide drop them into the torrent. A strong swimmer, he doubted his ability to make it across the storm-maddened flow alive. He had no idea whether Sister Angela could even swim— and, personal feelings aside, he needed her for the plan he was forming in the back of his mind.

Isolated in the saloon, Jessie, Coulter, the drunken British piano player Cordwainer, and a handful of dancing girls could not hold out long against the might of the enraged Temperance Army. And formidable as he was, he knew his arrival would not be nearly enough to turn the tide. Sister Angela was their only chance.

The bridge was right in front of them. Perhaps from safety-consciousness, perhaps from ostentation, the city fathers of Center City had flanked it with four-foot-high railings made of four-inch timbers hauled across the treeless prairie at substantial expense.

As they approached the bridge, a figure detached itself from the near endpost of the railing and stood up—and up, to loom against the clouds like a black colossus blocking the entrance to the bridge.

"You make it too easy, little man," a deep voice said in a heavy French accent. A lightning bolt tore a jagged line across the sky directly overhead, illuminating the face of LeClerc, his curly dark sideburns framing a wide-jawed smile. "I knew you would come this way. And now you and la petite chouette will die."

★

Chapter 18

"Here they come!"

Thunder cracked, so loud and immediate Jessie ducked, half-expecting the moan of a bullet past her head. She looked south to follow Tyrone McNair's outflung arm. Bobbing lanterns were coming north on Central past the square. As she watched more gleams resolved out of the rain, strung out along the street like an inchworm.

"Time to go," murmured David Coulter. She glanced at him, saw him looking at her, felt a warm flush creep up her cheeks in defiance of the chill sheets of rain. She wished she could grasp his hand, but that would be indiscreet. As it was, she was unsure what their allies made of their unfortunately brief absence. If they had drawn scandalous conclusions, they were minding their own business.

Tyrone went down the ladder into the second-story hallway so fast he barely touched the rungs. The youth was clearly eager for action. Jessie hoped his first taste would not also be his last.

"Will you be all right up here?" she asked McAllister and Dolphus Jefferson.

"Don't you worry yourself about us none," the black man said. He was unhurriedly unwrapping his Sharps, ignoring the miniature waterfall streaming from the front of his slouch hat brim.

McAllister waved his good arm. "We'll be fine. Watch yourselves."

Jessie poised on the verge of warning them not to open fire until an unmistakable attack was made on the saloon. She held her tongue. Both men were mature in behavior as well as years, showing no trace of the greenhorn buck fever that made young Tyrone vibrate like an arrow fresh-shot into a birch tree. She nodded and went past David, who stood courteously beside the open hatch to let her precede him.

As she passed he caught her hand for a quick, covert squeeze. She gave him a smile in return, and clambered down the ladder.

Down in the main room the saloon had the tensely expectant air of a besieged fortress. The big outer doors had been closed and locked over the double-hung saloon gate. Precious planks had been nailed over the inside of the doorway for additional protection against battering-rams, and the boards which already covered the windows had been checked to make sure they were fastened tightly.

With windows left and right, opening onto Central and Sullivan, and the doorway in the corner, the Liberty was not ideally set up for defense. Tables, chairs, upright piano had been pulled together into a barricade to the left of the hardwood bar. Neither would provide much defense against bullets, but they were better than nothing.

Double-barreled shotguns ready, Jessie and Tyrone crouched behind the bar. Coulter waited at the makeshift rampart, the bulky .32-caliber Merwin & Hulbert he had taken off the man who tried to shoot him that afternoon—a lifetime ago—in hand. Mr. Sylvester knelt beside him, his face pasty-pale in the lantern light, holding a shotgun as if afraid it might go off on its own accord at any second. His little Colt House pistol was safely tucked away in a pocket.

151

Martin Cordwainer was stationed in the pantry, cold sober and with all alcohol locked firmly away, to watch the back door. He had a single-barreled shotgun, but was mostly expected to give warning in case anybody started to break in from the alleyway.

Jessie glanced aside at David. He nodded and smiled. He seemed as cool as Dolphus Jefferson—as cool as Ki, whose lack Jessie keenly felt right about now. She still had questions in her heart about whether he was as tough a customer as he had proclaimed himself.

She sighed. Time would tell. And in truth she found it harder to believe the quietly self-effacing publisher was a braggart than to believe he was a seasoned fighting man.

Ki, Ki, where are you? she asked in her mind. Afternoon and evening had been a constant struggle to keep worry for him from distracting her. She had great confidence in his skills, and in particular his *ninja*-honed knack for escape and raw survival. But their opponents were treacherous and shrewd; they might have been smart enough to kill him out of hand once they lured him from the Liberty. The thought chilled her worse than the rain that still poured down unabated outside.

She had little time to worry about her companion and bodyguard. The thump of a thrown stone against the planks over the front window and an angry wordless murmur, like the storm sound magnified, announced the arrival of the Temperance Army.

"So," Ki said, "you brought none of your friends along to help you this time?" He assumed a shallow stance that offered good mobility, began to move purposefully forward, in the faint hope that the French Canadian might instinctively back up a step or two, and come out onto the bridge proper where the railing would constrict him.

The huge man uttered a laugh like pebbles shaken in a gold prospector's pan. "I need no friends to make an end of you, little man. I need not even kill you! I shall break your spine and prop you against the bridgepost, to let you watch while I pleasure your woman and drown her in the creek. At least she shall die with a smile on her lips!"

Ki had no more words to say. His opponent wasn't obliging him by giving ground. Ki kept advancing; the big man liked to kick, so Ki wanted to get inside, where LeClerc's long legs would give him no advantage.

As Ki came in range, LeClerc whipped his right foot up as if to front-kick. Ki brought his hands forward to block. The French Canadian instead brought his foot out, around, and in to slam the instep against the side of Ki's head.

Ki staggered back, slipped in half-liquid mud, sat down hard. Grinning like a zombie in the glare of a lightning flash, LeClerc skipped forward, foot upraised to stomp in Ki's ribs. Ki threw up a hand as if in a desperate attempt to block, then rolled over and scythed his right leg out in a sweep kick. It took LeClerc's planted foot behind the heel and slapped it right out from under him. The big man fell heavily with a splash and a crash and cracked his head on the planks of the bridge.

Instantly Ki was up on all fours, scrambling forward like a monkey. He swarmed up the bigger man, straddled him and began to piledrive punches into his face.

A hook punch from LeClerc's massive right fist caught Ki in the temple and filled the space behind his eyes with red sparks in blackness. Ki reeled, stunned. LeClerc brought his legs up, clamped his knees around Ki's neck and rolled violently sideways, hoping to snap the smaller man's neck. Instead, Ki threw himself the way LeClerc was taking him, spun himself free of the French Canadian's grasp and went rolling away across the wet, slick grass.

He rolled over, came up on one knee—in time to hear Sister Angela's cry of warning. It came too late. LeClerc had come skipping forward. He snapped a kick that caught Ki at the point of the jaw, sent fresh sparks exploding through his brain, and stretched him full-length on the grass of the riverbank with the top of his head in the water.

From outside came a rending crash. Jessie frowned, puzzled.

"They just wrenched loose the hitching post," David

153

Coulter said. "To use as a battering ram."

"Why ain't they shootin' from the roof?" Tyrone muttered.

"I hope they keep holding their fire," Jessie said, steadying her double-gun across the top of the bar. "I don't want this to come to killing if it doesn't have to."

A bang from the front door. It didn't so much as quiver. Another bang, and another.

"Need more'n that bitty pole to bust them doors in," Tyrone said in satisfaction.

The boards that covered the window to the right of the doors exploded inwards in a shower of splinters.

"Time to finish this," LeClerc grunted. He was picking his way down the slight incline to the verge of the rain-swollen river. Ki lay motionless on his back, eyes half-shut, arms outstretched, black hair trailing away in the water like kelp.

Beside Ki, LeClerc stopped and swung up his right foot, preparing to drive the heel down with crushing force into the fallen man's groin or belly. Coming suddenly to life, Ki rolled onto his right side, hooked his right foot behind LeClerc's down heel, and kicked his other foot into the giant's locked knee with all his force.

The joint popped with a sound like a clay jar hitting flagstone.

The giant bellowed in agony. As he fell into the weeds at the water's edge Ki picked himself up, moving a bit sluggishly, and ran back along the bank to collect Sister Angela.

She smiled at him. Then the clouds above them lit to a massive internal lightning discharge, and her cornflower blue eyes glanced past his shoulders and went wide.

Bangs hanging lank in his eyes, slablike jaw set against the agony, LeClerc was hopping forward after Ki on his one good leg. He swung his injured leg roundhouse. Taken totally by surprise, Ki barely managed to fling up an arm to block.

The ruined knee thumped against his forearm. The knee bent backward. LeClerc uttered a scream of agony and triumph as his lower leg, no longer moored to the rest of his body, came swinging around to strike Ki's temple with the foot.

Something on the French Canadian's shoe—a metal eyelet, a buckle—gashed Ki above the right eye. Blood streamed down his face, mingling with the driven rain, invading his eye socket and blinding him on that side.

It was enough that LeClerc, hopping forward again, was able to catch Ki on the left side of the head with a wild haymaker. Ki's head snapped around. The giant smashed a straight right into his face.

Ki staggered backward. Another left almost rocked him from his feet, but he got an arm in the way of the right-handed blow that followed, just as his right foot went back into the water.

It instantly began to slide down and out on mud and drowned grass, forcing him into involuntary splits. He flailed his arms for balance.

"Oh, God, Ki, he's got a knife!" he heard Sister Angela scream.

Something squat and massive struck the saloon floor in a welter of splintered planks, rolled toward the bar, rumbling like thunder. Sylvester ducked, emitting a whinny of terror. *A keg of nails!* Jessie realized. *They got a keg of nails from somewhere and tossed it through the window.*

Motion in the opening, a gleam of teeth and eyes and wet hair as someone tried to clamber in. "Get back!" Jessie yelled. "Get back or I'll shoot!"

A booted foot came through the hole the barrel had made. Jessie fired one barrel, aiming high so that the charge of buck knocked a hole through the wall above the window. There were sounds of violent scrambling, and suddenly the window was clear.

155

"Yellow-bellies," Tyrone cawed.

"Don't get cocky," Coulter warned him. "They won't stay discouraged long."

As if to prove him right, a kerosene lantern came sailing in through the broken window like a dim comet. It shattered on the floorboards. Coal oil spread out into a pool and instantly *whoomped* into blue and yellow flame.

LeClerc's arm was coming down in an arc, the metal fang of a knife glittering dully from his fist. Ki flung up his fists in a quick X, crossed at the wrists. He caught the descending arm at the wrist.

The impact drove him farther back down into the water. LeClerc twisted the knife down, gashing Ki's wrist. Ignoring the quick spike of pain, Ki grabbed LeClerc's knife arm, turned around, and jackknifed his body forward.

He was trying to throw the huge French Canadian over his shoulder. Poorly balanced as LeClerc was, with one good leg, Ki wasn't positioned well, didn't have the proper leverage. The big man fell on top of him.

The momentum of their two bodies somersaulted them both into the flood.

★

Chapter 19

"Damn!" Bern McAllister exclaimed. "That son of a bitch just threw a lantern into the saloon!"

"Guess it's time," Dolphus Jefferson said regretfully. With his thumb he drew back the Sharps' big side-hammer.

A moment later he saw a temperance soldier cock his arm to throw a second lantern. He squeezed the trigger.

The Sharps roared and kicked his shoulder. Down on Central, the would-be lantern hurler's head exploded to the impact of a .58-caliber bullet.

The *crump* of Dolphus Jefferson's Sharps echoed off the false fronts of the buildings across Central. Jessie heard a cry from the street, saw a flare of flame in the dark, quickly extinguished by the rain.

"Sally! Water!" Jessie cried. The black-haired dancing girl came scuttling out from the back room, holding a bucket of water. She tossed it over the puddle of flaming kerosene, which hissed and went out. She fled with the empty bucket as screaming temperance soldiers came lunging through the busted-in window.

157

Gritting her teeth, Jessie aimed dead-center of the window. Across the twin brass bead sights perched at the end of the long barrels she saw an expanse of blue plaid flannel shirt. *So be it,* she thought, and pulled one of the triggers.

Red splattered outward from the center of the shirt, as if a huge stone had been dropped in a pool of blood. Someone screamed. A double *bang* from hard nearby, and crystal shards and wax candle fragments rained down on Jessie's head.

Shaking her head to clear her eyes, she squeezed the second trigger. The shotgun bucked and roared, filling the dimly lit saloon with a yellow flash. A bearded howling face shattered in a spray of red and white.

The mob fell back. There were cries from the night of more than terror: it wasn't more than about seven yards from the bar to the window, and over such distance the charges from a shotgun with a full-length barrel didn't have much chance to spread, but several temperance soldiers had caught stray pellets, and were none too happy about it.

Jessie glanced around. At her side Tyrone was reloading with fingers that seemed skittish as a small frightened animal. A few yards away Sylvester knelt behind the makeshift barricade, his double gun broken open, fingers fumbling after cartridges he'd spilled on the planks. Eyes tight-shut, the shopkeeper had loosed off both barrels of his own shotgun—dead into the ceiling, accounting for the fall of debris on Jessie's head.

David Coulter was aiming his own unfired shotgun across the barrier, waiting coolly for the next onslaught. The fat-cylindered Merwin & Hulbert rested on the floorboards next to him. He looked at Jessie, sighed, shook his shaggy head, and showed her a taut grin.

"Now we see," he said, "whether we'd taken the heart out of them or just driven them crazy with the lust for revenge."

"Soldiers of the Temperance Army," a voice cried from outside, "hear me!"

"Uh-oh," Jessie murmured. "Sounds like my old friend Dan Brokaw."

"Our beloved Sister Angela dies this hour, defiled in her tent!" the former journalist screamed. "Yonder is the Jezebel responsible, cowering within her den of sin. What do you say, O soldiers of the Lord?"

"Kill!" the mob replied with a screech so mighty it seemed to make the downpour pause. The boards nailed over the door and the still covered window reverberated to the impact of charging bodies. From above came the sound of a revolver's six shots let off in firecracker succession, *bang-bang-bang*.

"Guess that gives us our answer," David Coulter said, and fired his shotgun into the mass of bodies that suddenly filled the broken window.

"Stirring oratory, Herr Brokaw," the baron said approvingly as Billy Dill reached up to help the small, big-headed man down from the buckboard from which he had made his appeal to the mob. Pappenheim had buckled a saber in a bright metal scabbard about his narrow hips. He looked altogether dashing, and not at all fazed by the downpour.

As Brokaw jumped down something hummed, knocked his bowler spinning from his head, and splintered the back of the light wagon's driver's seat. With a yell of surprised outrage he dropped flat into the sea of muck the rain had made of Center City's main street.

"Someone's on the roof," the baron said conversationally. "He just shot at you and missed."

Flashes through the broken window of the saloon, and shouts of pain, terror, and rage from the mob as it recoiled away from the opening yet again, showed that shooting was still going on inside as well.

Brokaw raised his head and spat out foul mud. "That son of a bitch!" he raged.

Billy Dill showed him a feral grin. "My boys can handle that. Same way they're fixing to open the door for us."

He gestured at a wagon parked about twenty yards farther

up the street. From the driver's seat of that wagon the Tucumcari Kid nodded. He stuck his cigar firmly in the corner of his mouth, turned, reached under a canvas cover, brought out a stick of dynamite with fuse already in place, and handed it to one of the handful of hired gunslingers Dill had brought with him.

"Roof," the stocky outlaw said. The gunslinger nodded, and trotted toward the saloon.

The Kid looked at the Liberty. Other hired guns were herding the mob back away from the still blocked door and the window which opened on Sullivan. The Kid's wagon faced that window, and looked to be well within the throwing range of his good right arm.

"No reason I can't have me some fun," he said to himself. He reached into the covered box for another stick.

Inside the saloon, the defenders heard a sudden thunderous *bang* and the several layers of the front door blew inward in a flash and a whirlwind of splinters. Jessie felt something sting her cheek. Belatedly she ducked.

On the roof, McAllister and Jefferson were trying to look everywhere at once. Holding his Winchester between his knees while he stuffed cartridges into the receiver with his one good hand, the stable owner suddenly broke off to point and caw hoarsely. "Look! That son of a bitch has got dynamite!"

Jefferson glanced along Central. A man stood in the driver's seat of a wagon, lighting a dynamite stick from a stub of a cigar, with his head tipped forward to shield the flame from the rain with his hat brim. Smoothly Jefferson raised the Sharps to his shoulder, drew bead, and fired.

As the Sharps fired his own world was enveloped in a blinding brilliance and vastly louder noise.

Dan Brokaw nodded in satisfaction. First that accursedly obdurate door was blasted from the path of the avenging Temperance Army. A heartbeat later a dynamite bomb exploded on the roof, which should certainly take care of the sharpshooters up there. Now all that remained should be a bloody rapid spasm, like a terrier shaking a rat.

"Get down," the baron said in a voice of no great urgency. In astonishment Brokaw saw the elegant Prussian nobleman fling himself face down in the mud the reporter had so recently climbed out of.

The act was sufficiently unexpected to impart some urgency to Pappenheim's suggestion. Without questioning why, Brokaw stretched himself full-length in the soupy morass once more.

An eyeblink later the stick of dynamite, its fuse burning vigorously despite the rain, which the Tucumcari Kid had dropped into the wagon when Dolphus Jefferson's bullet hit him in the breastbone went off. It took the rest of the dynamite sticks stacked in the covered box with it in a titanic eruption of noise and white light.

"What the blazes was that?" asked Tyrone, saucer-eyed.

There was more screaming out in the rain. Someone ran past on Central moaning, "My eyes, my eyes, Good God, my eyes!"

"Sounds like they've got a cannon out there," Jessie said.

Coulter shook his head. "Sound was too sharp." He sounded as if he were speaking from very far away, through the ringing in Jessie's ears. "That was dynamite. A fair amount of it."

She glanced his way. The right sleeve of his shirt was turning red above the elbow. She gasped. "You're hurt!"

"I'm fine. Just a splinter from the door blowing in." He nodded at her. "You might look to that cut on your cheek, by the way."

She raised one hand to her face. The fingers came away bright with blood. "Lemme help, there, Missy," Tyrone offered, digging in his pocket for a handkerchief.

"Don't mind me. Face cuts always look worse than they are. Best mind the door instead—because here they come again!"

• • •

His ears filled with a thin whining, Brokaw leapt up out of the mud while bits of the shattered wagon, and clumps of the unfortunate Tucumcari Kid, were raining down in the mud around him. He saw a tall skinny man with wild red whiskers lying on his back kicking up gouts of muddy water, writhing and clutching at a foot-long splinter of wood rammed through his neck. Brokaw swallowed, then sucked down a deep breath.

"It's the devil's work!" he roared. "Get after them, destroy them before they can set loose more imps of Satan!"

Raked by splinters, the street dotted with sprawled victims of the shooters inside and on top of the saloon, the mob had begun to waver. Already a few of those whose faith in the Lord was not so strongly tempered were taking to their heels, streaming away along Central, back in the direction of the largely abandoned Temperance Army camp.

Brokaw's cry roused the heartier survivors from their confused disorientation. They turned toward the saloon again. Billy Dill waved his hat and shouted at his men: "Git in there and take care of things! Git!"

One of the imported gunslingers drew his heavy Colt and charged through the gaping wound that had been the Liberty's front door.

Screaming like a mad thing, a figure burst into the saloon. Yellow flame blossomed from his hand. A soft lead bullet punched through the makeshift barricade and gouged a red furrow along Mr. Sylvester's well-padded short ribs.

Screaming his own shrill cry of pain and outrage the millinery store owner rose up from behind the barrier, his little pistol cracking furiously. A shot hit the intruder in the left shoulder, as much by accident as design.

The gunman cursed, aimed, and shot Sylvester through the forehead.

David Coulter came to one knee and shot the gunman

162

in the belly with his shotgun. The mob rushed in through the door and window. Coulter twitched his weapon right and fired the other barrel, cutting down two temperance soldiers, as Jessie and Tyrone emptied their own scatterguns.

Temperance soldiers slipped and fell in the blood and guts of their comrades that covered the planks in a red morass as treacherous as the mud outside. Coulter reversed his grip on the shotgun, clubbed down a black-haired youth who struck at him with a long knife.

Another figure in hat and duster coat appeared in the door, black against the rain, arm upraised to aim a long Remington revolver. Coulter snatched up the Merwin & Hulbert, pointed it, and pulled the trigger.

Nothing happened. The overly complicated mechanism had jammed.

The gunslinger laughed, cocked the hammer with his thumb. Coulter dove over the barricade, rolled toward him. The gunslinger fired, missed high. The publisher hit him in the legs and knocked him down.

Jessie had her double-gun broken open and was frantically trying to stuff fresh cartridges into the breech. A huge man with a scraggly moustache loomed up before her, grabbing at her. She snapped the weapon shut, poked it into the midst of his capacious belly, and fired. His huge gut exploded, showering her with gore and bits of tissue. He fell away, shirt afire from muzzle blast, as another temperance soldier grabbed the shotgun by its barrels. He cursed as he burned his hand, but tore the weapon right out of Jessie's hands.

Tyrone gave up trying to reload his weapon and lunged at the man. "Take that, you hellspawn nigger!" the temperance soldier snarled. He took a two-handed grip and struck Tyrone across the face with the shotgun's butt.

He turned to Jessie. She had the heavy-frame Smith & Wesson .38 her father had given her, cocked and leveled at his face. "Put the gun down and back away and you won't get hurt," she said in a drumhead-tight voice.

He guffawed. "Aw, you don't have the nerve—"

She shot him in the mouth. The crowd surging in behind him yelled and shied back as his brains splattered them. They hesitated a moment, but the force of other temperance soldiers crowding in behind them drove them forward at her.

The gun flew from the hired killer's hand when he hit the floor. He tried to grab hold of Coulter. The publisher slammed the heel of his palm up under his jaw, stunning him.

Coulter dove for the gun, which lay in the center of the floor, slowly rotating. He seized it, rolled, came up leveling it at the shattered door as a fresh wave of attackers flooded in.

The hammer of Jessie's double action clicked home on the empty cylinder with a chilling finality. Sensing that she was out of ammunition, the mob surged toward her with renewed fury. Twisted faces bellowed hate too savage for words—wordless promises of what the clawed fingers clutching for her across the bar would do when they got hold of her.

She ducked down behind the bar, evading the swipe of an arm. Tyrone lay at her side with blood streaming down his temple, stunned or even dead. She heard the revolver David had recovered firing frantically. Yellow-orange pulses of light lit the saloon.

Beneath the bar was an axe handle, which the bartender kept on tap for those social occasions on which the shotgun which was also customarily stashed there represented excessive force. She grabbed it, stood back up in time to slam it across the back of a hairy hand and crush it against the bar like a pale tarantula.

"You'll pay for that, harlot!" the hand's owner squalled. In her heart Jessie knew he was right.

A score or more of Temperance Army faithful were

inside, and others were pouring in from the street. The saloon air was choked with the humid smells of clothes and bodies drenched in rain and feverish sweat. Jessie cocked the axe handle over her shoulder.

So this is how it ends, she thought, her green eyes blazing defiance at the mob. *Oh, Ki, where are you?*

★

Chapter 20

"My children!" The voice cried out from the direction of the square. It pierced right through the clamor of the storm, feminine and clear and achingly familiar. "Soldiers of the Temperance Army, heed me!"

Heads turned; eyes narrowed to squint through the rain and dark. The cry went up: "Sister Angela! It's a miracle!"

Standing under a porch overhang along Central in the other direction from the square, not far from the smoldering wreckage of the Tucumcari Kid and his dynamite wagon, Joachim Heinrich Jürgen Maria, Freiherr von Trott zu Pappenheim allowed a brief look of petulance to spoil the classic lines of his face.

"Scheisse," he said.

Dan Brokaw clutched his arms with desperate fingers. "I thought you said your man could take that Chinaman?"

"On rare occasions I am incorrect in my judgments." With a metallic slither he drew his saber. "By the way, should you lay your hand upon my person again, I shall have it off at the wrist."

Brokaw snatched back his hand as if the baron had

166

suddenly turned red-hot. "We've got to *do* something."

"Sister Angela has always been your protégé and your project," the baron said. "I suggest you see to it."

"And you?"

Pappenheim held up his saber, turned it so that vagrant gleams of lantern light ran up its curved steel length like lover's fingers.

"I am going to ensure that something at least is saved from this shambles," he said, "by personally ending the life of Jessica Starbuck."

For a moment the occupants of the Liberty stood frozen in an odd tableau: Jessie standing behind the bar, axe handle poised like a baseball bat above her shoulder to strike at whichever temperance soldier first grew bold enough to break the deadlock; David Coulter backed against the wall, one hand wrapped in an attacker's grubby red plaid shirt, the other cocked to deliver a blow to his face; the mob, not quite ready to move in for the kill, sensing that these two were still capable of selling their lives quite dearly— and no temperance soldier eager enough for martyrdom to want to be one to pay the cost.

From the street outside were shouts, wild and elated. The members of the mob began to look at each other and exchange mutters: "It's Sister Angela! She ain't dead after all!"

The name rippled through the crowd like aftershocks of an earthquake: "Sister Angela! She's been returned to us. Praise be to God Almighty!"

The mob in front of the Liberty was already beginning to break up and stream back a block to where a tall, pale figure stood in the box of a buckboard which had been wheeled out of McAllister's Livery Stable.

"My faithful," Sister Angela was declaiming in her familiar brazen-lunged voice, "we have been deceived, you and I, by the very limbs of Satan! Leave off trying to harm the occupants of yon saloon, for they are blameless!"

"Damn!" muttered Brokaw. He spotted a trio of the hirelings Dill had brought in at his bequest, standing across Central from the Liberty, watching in bemusement as what had been a frantic lynch mob moments before turned into a milling, confused herd. He strode importantly up to them.

"The woman," he said. "Do something about her. But do it quietly—no guns."

The hired toughs looked at each other, shrugged, and moved off through the crowd.

Brokaw followed them. It was time he took an active hand in this. That comic-opera popinjay of a baron had, when all was said and done, made a terrific botch of things. It was up to Dan Brokaw, now, as a man who was schooled as a reporter and therefore knew how the world *really* worked, to take the situation in hand.

Already much of the mob had coalesced around the wagon on which the evangelist stood, staring raptly upwards at her rain-soaked, lantern-lit figure. She seemed to be wearing nothing but a flowery blanket pulled about her. She showed a long gleaming expanse of thigh, and one breast hung free like an especially ripe and succulent fruit, which might have helped account for the crowd's absorption.

Though he was a man of the world and above animal temptation, the sight quickened Brokaw's heart and pulled it up into his throat. *She should by rights belong to me,* he thought. He felt a stir of regret at what had to happen. Then he realized that his mind was sufficiently nimble that he could handle this without any harm having to come to the beautiful blond evangelist.

When I get the crowd straightened out and once more headed in the proper direction . . . we shall just see what happens. He raised his hands.

"Faithful soldiers of the Temperance Army," he declaimed, "I rejoice with you that our Sister has been returned to us. But the terrible events which have befallen her have temporarily unhinged her—"

Sister Angela pointed a shaking finger at him, causing the blanket to fall open further. "There he is!" she screamed.

"The limb of Satan who used me, betrayed me—and sought to kill me!"

Lightning blazed overhead. With an angry animal growl that seemed to grow out of the thunder's rumble, the crowd turned toward Brokaw. "Wait," he said, holding up his hands and beginning to backpedal. "This is all a terrible misunderstanding. You all know me—"

He looked from face to face. He saw nothing resembling pity or forbearance. He tried desperately to match names to known faces, could not. He had never troubled himself to pay much attention to the rank and file of the Temperance Army. They were too lowly to concern him.

"You all know me," he settled for repeating plaintively. "I'm Sister Angela's greatest friend and supporter. I'd never—"

"Do not listen to him," Sister Angela commanded. "Like the Serpent, he seduced me with his honeyed words."

The lovely sister meant that metaphorically. Possibly the crowd didn't take it that way. With a great scream of outrage it lunged forward.

"Wait, now, w-w-ait!" Brokaw stammered as harsh hands were laid upon him. "Don't do anything to imperil your immortal souls! I'm under the Lord's protection."

A blow caught him across his face. He gaped at the pain, at the unfamiliar sensation of blood streaming over his upper lip. "You *swine!*" he screamed.

They rushed upon him, grabbing, twisting, pulling. Dan Brokaw was lifted into the air, pulled spread-eagle, stretched. He cursed them until a burly mechanic grabbed his lantern-like lower jaw and tore it from his face with a heave and a geyser of blood.

Brokaw screamed without the benefit of words as the crowd tore him limb from limb.

"My God," Sister Angela said, "what have I done?"

"Nothing," Ki said, reaching up to pat her hand reassuringly. "*They're* doing it."

He looked into her eyes. "You'll be safe here, among

your people. Now I must go to my employer."

She nodded numbly. He turned away.

The first thing he saw was three men in cowboy hats converging on the wagon like wolves upon a strayed buffalo calf.

The mob had vanished from the Liberty like the tide going out, leaving a flotsam of at least a dozen bodies, bullet-torn and trampled, lying in their blood on the floor. Jessie's eyes met Coulter's across the carnage.

"Sister Angela appears to have returned," the editor said. "And somehow she seems to be on our side."

"What makes me think Ki is behind this somehow?"

He grinned, then knelt down to rifle the pockets of the gunman he'd stunned, who had gotten rolled up against the wall beneath the still boarded-over window that opened onto Sullivan. The man stirred, rolled over, striking out at Coulter. The lanky editor stunned him again with a hammerfist blow to the temple, and returned to rummaging for fresh ammunition for the gun he'd emptied during the mob's final charge.

Jessie knelt to examine young Tyrone. The boy was still dazed and bleeding from the blow to the head. She thumbed back his eyelids. His pupils were both the same size. "Good," she said. "No concussion, anyway. With a little luck we'll have you back on your feet in no time."

"Guten Abend," a cultured voice said from the door.

Jessie and David looked up to see Baron von Pappenheim standing there with a saber naked in his hand.

One of the hired killers, with a red bandanna around his neck and a knife in his hand, was closer than the others. He showed a loose-lipped grin as Ki glided toward him.

"Come and git some, slant-eyes," he said, making beckoning gestures with his left hand.

Ki kept advancing. The man's eyes got wide. He slashed at Ki's face. Ki leaned lithely back. The blow cut air half an inch from his eyes.

He leaned forward. The man slashed at him again. Once more he slipped the cut without apparent effort, then took a shuffling step forward and snapped a vertical fist against the man's nose.

Blood squirted from the killer's nostrils. "Ow!" he shrilled. "Why, you mealy yellow son of a bitch!"

He lunged forward, stabbing for Ki's washboard belly. Ki caught his wrist and went to one knee, turning and drawing the arm over his shoulder as he did so. When the man's elbow was locked-out tight and balanced on the fulcrum of Ki's shoulder bone, he pulled down on the wrist with savage force.

The man's arm bent backwards to ninety degrees as his elbow broke with a splintering crack. He howled.

The knife fell from useless fingers. Ki let go of the ruined arm and scooped up the knife, holding it blade downwards. With the speed of a striking prairie rattler he turned and jammed the point down through the top of the outlaw's skull as the man stood clutching his elbow.

"Ki! Behind you!" Sister Angela cried—a heartbeat too late, as strong arms seized Ki's biceps from behind. A fist drove into his kidneys with a force that caused purple lightning to flare behind his eyelids. His knees buckled and he dropped to his knees in the water that filled a rut in the street.

Coulter skipped away from the young Prussian, three quick long-legged steps that took him to the door of the pantry where the dancing girls were cowering. He held out a hand. "Broom," he commanded.

The baron did not advance. He merely stood and watched the publisher's antics with a sneer of amused contempt twisting his fine thin lips.

After a moment's confusion a broom was thrust out of the pantry and into Coulter's outstretched hand. He took it in two hands by the handle, holding the head angled up from his waist as he approached the baron.

"Do you seriously expect to challenge me with that

171

ridiculous toy?" Pappenheim asked.

Coulter showed his long, horsy teeth in a grin. "Try me."

The baron shrugged. "Very well."

Without warning, his saber whipped around in a figure eight. There was a *clack* of impact, and the head of the broom went spinning free.

★

Chapter 21

A hand gripped the hair at the front of Ki's head from behind, hauling him bodily back to his feet.

"We're gonna make you sorry for the way you stuck that knife in our pal, Chinaman," a voice hissed in his left ear in a gust of foul breath.

"Yeah," a voice said from his other side. "And maybe the old baron'll let us have a little bit of that Starbuck bitch afore he goes slittin' her throat."

Ki snapped his left fist up, thumb extended. He felt a moment of resistance, then a pop as it plunged into the eye of the man who held him by the hair.

The man uttered an unearthly screech and released him. Ki whipped his other hand up in a backfist into the face of the startled outlaw on that side. That man let go and took two steps backwards.

"Damn this noise," he muttered, and dropped his hand to his six-gun.

Ki skipped forward, seized his gunhand by the wrist before he could draw, and slammed his right elbow into the man's temple. The gunman wobbled. Ki brought his knee up hard into his crotch, and as he doubled over took his head in both hands and hauled it sharply down to meet a rapidly rising knee.

Ki turned. The man with the burst eyeball was weeping tears from his remaining eye and trying to haul out his own gun. Before he could bring it to bear, Ki took three quick steps and knocked it from his hand with a straight-legged crescent kick from his right leg. Without dropping the leg he snapped his foot back the other way, catching the one-eyed man on the bloody side of his face and sending him back a few unsteady steps.

Ki did a rapid side-step and fired a side-kick into the gunman's midriff. The man flew backward against the wagon on which Sister Angela, the blanket forgotten and now slumped mostly away to reveal almost all her considerable charms, still stood. He cracked his head against the steel rim of one wheel and slumped.

Ki looked toward the saloon. "Jessie!" he gasped, and began to run.

When Pappenheim decapitated the broom Jessie dropped immediately to all fours behind the bar, looking for reloads for either her .38 or the shotguns. To her horror she found the boxes of cartridges had somehow gotten kicked away in the fighting and were nowhere to be seen.

She seized a shotgun, jumped up, and aimed it at the baron. "Drop the toadsticker, Joachim!" she commanded.

He looked at her and laughed. "The hammers are down," he observed. "I really think you're bluffing, dear lady."

She scowled, lowered the piece. Davey spun the shortened broomstick and dropped into what looked suspiciously like an Oriental fighting stance, with the broom tucked under his right arm and his advanced left arm raised in a guard position.

"What is this?" the baron asked. "Do you still think to resist me?"

"Come and get me," Coulter said, "if you can."

The baron shrugged—and turned the motion into a

stamping lunge as he delivered an overhand cut at the publisher's head.

The staff swirled, caught the side of the long curved blade as it descended, steered it harmlessly down the left side of Coulter's body. Then it spun back up to crack Pappenheim across the side of the face before he could recover.

He jumped back, bringing the sword swiftly back en garde. With his left hand he felt the side of his face as Coulter settled back into his own ready stance, broomstick held before him like a two-handed sword once more.

"A good staff man's at no disadvantage against a swordsman, mein Herr," David Coulter said. "A man armed with a five-foot staff was the only opponent ever to beat Miyamoto Musashi—whom I doubt you've heard of, but who was the finest swordsman who ever lived."

Pappenheim examined the blood on his fingertips. His smile was not pleasant. "I suggest you save your breath for screaming, my friend," he said, and attacked.

The sheer fury of his onslaught forced the young publisher back to the makeshift barrier. Still, Coulter parried every stroke of the saber, never meeting blade-edge with the wood of his staff. When his heel struck the barricade, the baron's eyes widened in triumph. He beat the broomstick aside and thrust for Coulter's belly.

Coulter threw himself to the right, out of harm's way. The baron found himself draped over a table turned on its side, looking down at Sylvester's corpse.

A lit kerosene lamp sat beside the body. Pappenheim grinned, stuck the tip of his saber through the handle, and flipped the lantern through the air at Jessie, who was still standing behind the bar holding the shotgun in her hands.

The glass of the lamp broke almost at her feet. Kerosene spilled out, burning with it a blue highlight. Jessie cried out as the stuff splashed her legs of her jeans and set them alight.

"Something to think about, Fräulein," Pappenheim said with a grin, and spun to face Coulter.

Jessie dove headfirst across the bar, tucked her shoulders

175

as she hit the floorboards, and rolled. She bumped against a corpse. A rain-sodden slouch hat lay beside it. She grabbed it and used it to beat the flames on her lower legs.

Advancing with crisp steps, the baron made a forehand cut at Coulter's eyes, and when it was parried, whipped the blade around for a backhand stroke. That was blocked, too. Pappenheim reared back, stabbed suddenly for Coulter's thigh. The stick whipped down to deflect the thrust.

It was a feint. Instantly Pappenheim withdrew the sword, and then poked it into Coulter's left biceps.

Jessie, who had just managed to douse the flames, cried out in alarm.

Coulter danced back. "And that's one for you, Freiherr," he said.

"And no time to finish this travesty," Pappenheim said. The hardwood bar was truly aflame now, burning with a crackling roar to challenge the cloudburst outside. From the back rooms came cries of alarm.

"Indeed." Coulter thrust the broomstick right at the baron's face. The saber clacked against it.

Coulter was already in motion, spinning widdershins into the youthful Prussian and slamming the butt of the staff into Pappenheim's belly. The baron bent over, but jumped back, trying to draw the saber back for another stroke.

Coulter brought the broomstick whistling down across Pappenheim's forearm. The saber dropped from suddenly limp fingers and rang on the blood-slick planking like a fine silver bell. With the return stroke Coulter smashed the stick across the baron's face, and caught him a second shot to the head as he flew backwards into the wall.

Coulter tucked the broomstick back under his arm in a ready stance and stood waiting. "Had enough, Freiherr?"

The baron stirred feebly, then opened his eyes. They were startling blue in his bloody mask of a face.

"In a manner of speaking," he said, and raised his right arm. A two-shot .44 derringer protruded from his fist. Coulter turned and dove headlong over the barricade.

A large object came flying in the open window, unrolled

with a thump of bare feet on wood. "Jessie!" Ki called. "Are you all ri—"

Snarling, Pappenheim turned the little hideout pistol on Ki. Jessie reared up from behind a sprawled corpse and threw her shotgun. The barrel cracked against the bones of the baron's wrist. The little gun flew from his hand.

Ki grinned and kicked Pappenheim in the face. The baron was slammed against the wall. He planted his feet and whipped himself upright like a jack-in-the-box.

Ki punched him in the face. The handsome head rocked back. Ki snap-kicked him in the belly, then rushed him, pinning the dashing young nobleman to the wall and ramming his knee into his side again and again.

"Ki!" Jessie cried. Holding the baron with a forearm bar across the throat, Ki turned his head. Two men had stepped into the now burning saloon. Each held a cocked six-gun, and both were pointed right at Ki.

"Step back away from the baron, Chinee," Billy Dill suggested in a conversational voice, "so's I can put a bullet in your belly."

David Coulter came flying back over the barricade in a wild leap. He hit the floor almost in the middle of the large barroom and rolled.

When he came up he had the baron's little derringer in one hand, and the other wrapped around it for support.

The derringer went off with the gigantic flash and thunderclap sound of all such short-barreled weapons. Billy Dill stood for a moment gazing at the publisher, eyes wide around the neat round hole that had appeared in his forehead.

As he collapsed bonelessly to the floor Coulter rolled to face the other gunman and fired again. The man grunted as the bullet took him in the gut. Still he held onto his Peacemaker, tried to raise it to shoot Coulter.

Coulter bounded to his feet. In a flash he was at the gunman's side, seizing his gunhand and bending it inward toward the outlaw's body. One finger forced its way inside the trigger guard, over the would-be assassin's finger.

The man's body muffled the sound of the shot.

· · ·

The unexpected turn of events had distracted Ki. He felt a sudden stab of agony in his side and stepped back, letting the baron go.

The young Prussian had a small knife in his left hand. He grabbed Ki by the chin and made to slash his throat.

Behind Ki, Coulter wrested the big pistol from the dying gunman's hand. He whipped it up, cocking it as he raised it, and fired past Ki's shoulder without seeming to aim.

The bullet smashed Pappenheim's left shoulder. He dropped the knife.

The baron shoved Ki at Coulter, took two running steps, and dove out the window.

"Are you all right?" Coulter asked, catching Ki.

Ki felt his side. "The wound is not serious," he said. "Do you wish to pursue—"

"Tyrone!" Jessie yelped. "Oh my God, he's still behind the bar!"

Much of the rear of the saloon was involved in the fire now, but only about half the bar. Ki ran toward the safe end, leapt up on the bar, dropped on the far side. Coulter came up as Ki stood with the still unconscious youth draped over his shoulder, and took him and hauled him to safety.

The youth's clothes were smoldering. Coulter laid him on the floor. Jessie knelt beside him and began to beat out the fire as Ki vaulted back over the bar.

"We must get out of here," Ki said.

Jessie looked up. The flames were beginning to climb the banister now. She nodded, then grabbed one of Tyrone's arms to help haul him into the street.

They gathered in Central as the Liberty burned: Jessie, Ki, David, and Tyrone; Martin Cordwainer and the dancing girls, pale-faced but none the worse for wear, had escaped out the back. And here to Jessie's enormous relief came McAllister and Dolphus Jefferson, each supporting the other.

"Dynamite stunned us," Jefferson explained. "When we

come to, the place was burning mighty pretty."

"Lucky for us we could shinny down the rain gutter," McAllister said.

Jessie embraced the two men. Jefferson looked past her and his face went grim in the flamelight. "Tyrone—"

"He's fine, sir," said Coulter, who was kneeling beside the youngster. "Just took a nasty crack on the head and breathed some smoke. But he should recover nicely."

A few scattered remnants of the Temperance Army stood around in the pouring rain looking lost. The majority had vanished—probably back to their homes, where they'd try to forget what had happened tonight, most likely with the substantial help of their erstwhile foe, the Demon Rum.

Of Baron von Pappenheim there was no sign. Since his unmistakable black stallion was also missing, the general consensus was that he had mounted up and ridden off into the storm-wracked plains. Jessie hoped he'd bleed to death, but doubted she would be that lucky. The young snake was too tough for that, for all his well-oiled Continental elegance.

One by one the townspeople of Center City turned out to form a bucket brigade to fight the fire. "I thank you all," Jessie told them, "but it's too late for the Liberty. Just make sure the fire doesn't spread."

"Miss Starbuck."

She turned. Sister Angela stood there, her glorious blond hair matted to her head, the wet coverlet clutched about her lush body and not really concealing that much of it. Still, she managed to look mighty regal, Jessie had to admit.

"Sister Angela," she said.

"I have done you a power of hurt, Miss Starbuck," the evangelist said. "I know words are sorry things at a time like this, but—I'm sorry."

For a moment Jessie stared at her. Then she gave a little laugh and shook her head.

"Yes," she said. "You've done a lot of hurt to me and mine. But Ki tells me you were being manipulated by that little polecat Brokaw. And besides, you did save our lives

179

there at the end. So I reckon that squares us."

"Ki opened my eyes to what Brokaw was doing," the evangelist breathed, "and to so much besides."

She moved to his side, put her arm around him. "Now I see how wrongheaded my crusade was. Many people do themselves harm with drink, but that is between the Lord and them; ' "Vengeance is mine," said the Lord.' In my pride, I thought to usurp the Lord's prerogative of judging."

"So you're out of the crusading business?" David Coulter asked with interest.

She smiled sweetly. "Out of the temperance business; I now see it's a sin to try to tell people how to run their lives."

She stroked Ki's arm. "Ki showed me . . . well, he gave me much to think about. I hope you and he aren't leaving too soon?"

Jessie shook her head. "I'm going to see the Liberty rebuilt first."

"Oh, *good*," Sister Angela practically squealed. "Then Ki can teach me more of those marvelous Eastern secrets! And then I think I'll go to Boston and look into Victoria Woodhull's Free Love movement."

"Miss Starbuck."

"That name is on everybody's lips tonight," Jessie said. She turned to see a stout figure approaching down Central from the square.

"Chief Coates," she said, in an oddly neutral voice.

The town police chief nodded. He wore full dress uniform, complete with double row of brass buttons gleaming on his tunic and a leather policeman's helmet perched on his head.

"People of Center City," he said loudly, "behold how once again law and order are restored to our fair community. The moral is crystal clear: trust in your duly constituted moral authorities, and the forces of anarchy and chaos cannot harm you! Once again, your fearless police force has—"

Jessie tapped him on the shoulder. "Chief?"

He turned. "Did you have something on your mind, Miss Starbuck?"

"Only this," she said, and belted him in the face with a right cross that sat him down on his broad blue-clad bottom in three inches of water. The crowd burst into applause.

"Just that," she said, and turned away.

She felt a warm presence at her side and looked up to see David Coulter grinning down at her. "Good right hand," he said.

Hiding her hands between their bodies, she rubbed her right with her left. "Stupid, though. Daddy taught me never to hit a man in the head with a closed fist. No, don't turn away! Ki will nag me forever if he sees."

"All right."

"You turn out to be a pretty fair hand with a shooting iron, too, by the way," she said. "Did you pick that up in that Chinese village, too?"

He laughed quietly, shook his head. "When I came back to the States, I joined the Pinkertons. I learned to handle a gun when I was with them."

She raised her eyebrows. "Oh, really? Why did you and the Eye that Never Sleeps part company?"

"I was involved in the Molly Maguire investigations a couple of years ago," he said. "I was pretty thoroughly disgusted both by union terrorism and the obvious railroading of those eleven Maguires they hanged. I figured, a plague on both houses. About that time was when I stumbled across the writings of Lysander Spooner. So I quit the agency, took my modest inheritance, and headed west to devote myself to spreading the doctrines of classical liberalism."

She shook her head. "You never cease to amaze me, Davey," she said. "What other surprises do you have in store for me?"

"None tonight," he said.

The saloon collapsed with a grumbling sigh and a skyward shower of sparks, quickly drowned by the rain. Coulter slipped his arm around Jessie's shoulders and they turned to look.

"One good thing," she said. "With all this rain, it looks as if they're not having any trouble keeping the blaze from spreading."

He nodded. "We don't need to stand here all night in the rain," he said. "Come to my house; I suspect you could use a good night's sleep."

"Sleep would be good," She smiled up at him. "But not just yet, if you don't mind?"

Arm and arm they walked off down the street.

A special offer for people who enjoy reading the best 'Westerns published today.

WESTERNS!

NO OBLIGATION

Mail the coupon below

To start your subscription and receive 2 FREE WESTERNS, fill out the coupon below and mail it today. We'll send your first shipment which includes 2 FREE BOOKS as soon as we receive it.

Mail To: **True Value Home Subscription Services, Inc. P.O. Box 5235**
120 Brighton Road, Clifton, New Jersey 07015-5235

YES! I want to start reviewing the very best Westerns being published today. Send me my first shipment of 6 Westerns for me to preview FREE for 10 days. If I decide to keep them, I'll pay for just 4 of the books at the low subscriber price of $2.75 each; a total $11.00 (a $21.00 value). Then each month I'll receive the 6 newest and best Westerns to preview Free for 10 days. If I'm not satisfied I may return them within 10 days and owe nothing. Otherwise I'll be billed at the special low subscriber rate of $2.75 each; a total of $16.50 (at least a $21.00 value) and save $4.50 off the publishers price. There are never any shipping, handling or other hidden charges. I understand I am under no obligation to purchase any number of books and I can cancel my subscription at any time, no questions asked. In any case the 2 FREE books are mine to keep.

Name _____

Street Address _____ Apt. No. _____

City _____ State _____ Zip Code _____

Telephone _____

Signature _____
(if under 18 parent or guardian must sign)

Terms and prices subject to change. Orders subject
to acceptance by True Value Home Subscription
Services. Inc.

11529-0